The Light of Love

Prayer is an uplifting of the heart, spirit, and soul, whatever you like to call it, and it happens, not at the specified times we choose, but a hundred times a day, often without us being consciously aware of it.

In this book I have set down for every day words which uplift ME. I pray that one or two may help stimulate thought and inspire you.

With these words, a world-famous writer introduces a diary of hope and love and life. Under each day's date is an entry: a short quotation from such writers as Emerson or Shaw, a bit of verse from Elizabeth Barrett Browning or William Blake, an extract from the Bible, a speech from a Shakespearean play. Accompanying the material is a comment by Barbara Cartland herself, describing the feeling that such thoughts awaken in her.

"It is the friendship of one's fellowmen which matters most," she writes on one winter's day. "The handclasp when one is afraid, the encouraging word when in doubt, the comfort and kindness in sorrow, and the warm companionship at all times."

"Conscience is something we can never lose. It is the voice of our soul."

Sorrow, joy, hope, despair, friendship, kindness, humor, the seasons with their mystic appeal to the human psyche—all these Miss Cartland talks about and through them reaches out to readers who want to share with her a profound sense of beauty and love that life has to offer.

BARBARA CARTLAND

The Light of Love

Lines to Live by
Day by Day

ELSEVIER/NELSON BOOKS
New York

Library of Congress Cataloging in Publication Data
Main entry under title:
The light of love.
1. Devotional calendars.   I. Cartland, Barbara,
1902–
BV4810.L48   242'.2   79–20929
ISBN 0–525–66654–0

*Published in the United States by Elsevier/Nelson Books,
a division of Elsevier-Dutton Publishing Company, Inc.
New York.*

Printed in the U.S.A. First Edition
10   9   8   7   6   5   4   3   2   1
Book Design by Ellen LoGiudice

Acknowledgments

Thanks are due to the following for permission to include copyright poems and quotations:
The Bodley Head for the poem by Walt Whitman from *Complete Poetry, Selected Prose and Letters;*
G.T. Sassoon for "Music of whispering trees . . ." by Siegfried Sassoon;
Macmillan, Inc., and The Society of Authors as the literary representative of the Estate of John Masefield for the extract from "Sea-fever";
Monica Furlong for the extract from her prayer "Dear God, it is so hard for us not to be anxious"; and
Macmillan Publishers Ltd. (and Vanguard Press) for the last stanza of "Holiday" by Edith Sitwell from *Collected Poems*, and for the extract from the works of Rabindranath Tagore.

Despite diligent inquiry some copyright holders have proved impossible to trace, and to them the author and publisher extend their most sincere apologies.

Introduction

We all want to find the World behind the World; we all want to step through the Looking Glass; we all want the security of knowing we are not alone and that death is not the end. It is so easy to say you must have faith, but difficult to be sure.

What we really seek is a link with God and that, the Church has told us for two thousand years, is prayer. But it took me a long time to realize that prayer is not just a formula of words, or a begging-bowl for our needs, but something far more esoteric and wonderful.

Prayer is an uplifting of the heart, spirit, and soul, whatever you like to call it, and it happens, not at the specified times we choose, but a hundred times a day, often without our being consciously aware of it.

Every time we feel that quick uplift within us at the sight of beauty, at the sound of music, or a note in someone's voice—that is prayer—

Sunshine on still water, the breeze in the trees, leafless branches against a winter sky, and in the passing of a second I am with them and it is a prayer.

A sympathetic smile from a stranger in a crowded bus, the welcome home from a child, the call of a loved one's voice—the glow it gives one is prayer.

The pain we feel at other people's suffering, at injustice, at cruelty is a prayer for them and for restitution.

We have, in rare and precious moments in our lives, flown on the wings of ecstasy and known the beauty and the glory of the Divine. But there are millions of other tiny, fleeting seconds when we reach with a sudden rapture upward and outward toward a distant horizon we sense but cannot see.

Almost before we realize it has happened, the wonder has passed, and yet we have actually touched what intrinsically is the Godhead.

In this book I have set down for everyday words which uplift *Me*. They may do nothing for you, although I pray that one or two may help, stimulate your thoughts, and inspire you.

We were created with eyes to see and ears to hear, but we limit our vision and dull our hearing because we forget we were also given a sixth sense. It is called intuition, and it is that which transforms the commonplace and the mundane into the esoteric.

Whether we know it or not, it is instinctive within us all to lift our souls toward the Infinite.

B.C.

The Light of Love

January

January 1

One thing I know, life can never die,
Translucent, splendid, flaming like the sun,
Only our bodies wither and deny
The life-force when our strength is done.

Let me transmit this wonderful fire,
Even a little through my heart and mind,
Bringing the perfect love we all desire
To those who seek, yet blindly cannot find.

January 2

As we get older we cling to our friends, those who have known us for many years, by whose side we have developed and changed and suffered. Those friendships are the real prizes we gain in the world-school in which we seek experience. So many work for the "glittering prizes"—titles, wealth, power, and social advancement; but these things are only a transitory pleasure and by no means an undiluted one.

They bring added responsibilities, difficulties, problems, and both head- and heartaches in their train. They can also bring a vast and empty loneliness unless they have been achieved in a spirit of love and unselfishness.

At the end of one's life, and indeed all through it, it is the friendship of one's fellow men which matters most. The handclasp when one is afraid, the encouraging word when in doubt, the comfort and kindness in sorrow, and the warm companionship at all times.

January 3

We see the world piece by piece, as the sun, the moon, the animal, the tree, but the whole, of which these are the shining parts, is the soul.

RALPH WALDO EMERSON

January 4

Memories, however golden, cannot fill an empty place—a home that is suddenly quiet, a desk at which no one sits, a silence which remains unbroken by a voice. I kept expecting, after he was killed, to see my brother Ronald come into the room, to hear him say: "What do you think, darling . . . ?" to meet him striding round the corner in his quick, unhesitating manner.

I tried to feel him near me, to pierce the barriers which divided us, to be convinced that he was there. That is, I believe, the real hindrance: our desire to be convinced logically, to know in a physical sense that those whom we cannot see are close. We strain, strive, listen and grasp at them with our bodily senses . . . it is our spiritual senses we must use—often undeveloped and unformed from years of disuse.

January 5

God be thanked, the meanest of His creatures
Boasts two soul-sides, one to face the world with,
One to show a woman when he loves her!

ROBERT BROWNING

Love makes us give our highest and our best to those we love.

January 6

When you loved me I gave you the whole sun and stars to play with. I gave you eternity in a single moment, strength of the mountains in one clasp of your arms, and the volume of all the seas in one impulse of your soul.

GEORGE BERNARD SHAW

It is significant and fascinating that we always want to give the person we love what God gives us.

January 7

I have always prayed. At first, because I was brought up by my mother to do so; later, because prayer in its simplest and often inarticulate form seems to come to me at all moments of emotion, and especially when I am moved by anything beautiful or mysterious.

All that is mystic has always attracted me, and I find it in unexpected places. The prayer that comes at such a moment is like a release; one feels an outward surge, a sudden breathless lifting of the spirit, as if it might conceivably move from out of the confines of the heavy body.

One waits—knowing this is only the preliminary to a moment of illumination, a merging and immersing within the whole pattern of creation. Almost invariably the moment passes—it was only a prayer, not a spiritual experience.

And yet, how immensely satisfying! Prayer is not only a petition—it is a movement of the soul.

January 8

The lover of life holds life in his hand,
 like a ring for the bride,
The lover of life is free of dread;
The lover of life holds life in his hand,
 As the hills hold the day.

       GEORGE MEREDITH

How often we forget in our preoccupation with other loves to love life. This love is the joy in the light of the rising sun, in the first buds of Spring, the white snow on the hills and the song of the birds.

 It is the thrill when we feel health pulsating through us and the strength to do just a little bit more than we have done before.

January 9

Bravery always touches me very deeply. A great friend of mine had a son called Donald, who, aged seventeen, and in the Royal Navy, was badly hurt in the raid on the Norwegian aerodrome of Stavanger in April 1940. An aircraft carrier and five destroyers were lost; while the other warships, including the cruiser which Donald was on, were subjected to continuous air attack the whole way back to port.

 When my friend went to see her son in hospital, the Surgeon said to her: "The one thing which is worrying him is that you will be so horrified at his appearance."

 It was terrifying to see her boy with his face black with anti-burn grease, his hair and eyelashes burnt away, his lips swollen until he could barely speak.

 "Was it awful, darling?" she asked, hardly conscious of what she was saying.

 "It was rather like being in a film," he answered, and then, with a flash of incorrigible humour, "without the love interest, of course!"

January 10

First time he kissed me, he but kissed the fingers of this hand whencewith I write and ever since, it grew more clear and white.

ELIZABETH BARRETT BROWNING

This is what love does for us! Because we love we want everything we do to be better, purer, more beautiful in every way. For Love is God working through us.

January 11

How little we value the miracle of speech! The Egyptians claimed that sound had the power of life and death; the Japanese have a special Yoga which by sound recalls a spirit which has already left the body. But for the ordinary man and woman speech is miraculous in itself; not only can we ask for what we want, we can explain, clarify and interpret our own thoughts and feelings to ourselves.

That is what is so important, to understand ourselves. And what is more, speech used by a Master mind can inspire and direct the strength which lives within us all. That strength which we draw from Life itself—or in simple words, from the Godhead.

January 12

The Angel that presided o'er my birth
Said, "Little Creature, formed of joy and Mirth,
Go love without the help of anything on Earth."

WILLIAM BLAKE

January 13

The sun, the moon, the stars, the hills and the plains,
Are not these, O Soul, the vision of Him who reigns?
The ear of man cannot hear, and the eye of man cannot
see;
But if we could see and hear this vision—were it not
He?

ALFRED, LORD TENNYSON

January 14

A Hungarian gypsy song says, "Love is like a rough sea,
you must surrender to its strength and majesty. It may
destroy you but you can never withstand it."

*Love will come to us whether we seek it or run away. Love is
invincible, omnipotent, unconquerable. Who can deny love?*

January 15

Lighten our darkness, we beseech thee, O Lord; and by
Thy great mercy defend us from all perils and dangers of this
night; for the love of thy only Son, our Saviour Jesus Christ.

*This prayer I say always when I am sleeping in a house where there
are ghosts, and if I wake in the night and feel frightened. I am always
so glad I learnt it when I was a child, and it has been there to help me
all through my life.*

17

January 16

I often told my mother that she made me "feel good" and by that I don't mean a nebulous, negative desire to be holy, but a strong impulse to be wiser, finer, and more creative. She had that amazing faculty of stripping away without words or criticism the cheap wrapping with which we all clutter ourselves, and finding the true self beneath.

That should be the real criterion of friendship—we seek in those we love as much perfection as there is in us. We are often too greedy; we ask so much of friends while giving so little. We all long for a confidante; it is a germ within every one of us that we like to lay our souls bare and to be absolutely honest with someone we love. But we have also to listen, to give as well as to gain. We should also have a sense of responsibility towards our friends. How often do we hear:

"Oh, I don't see much of her nowadays, she's deteriorated frightfully."

"I'm afraid old Bill's gone to the dogs."

"We haven't much in common now—she's got into such a rut."

Could we have prevented these things? Wasn't our influence, had we chosen to exert it, strong enough to save those who once meant so much in our lives from drifting away?

January 17

Labour to keep alive in your breast that little spark of celestial fire, called conscience.

GEORGE WASHINGTON

Conscience is something we can never lose. We try to do so, we ignore it and attempt to muzzle it, but it is still there. It is the voice, or rather the prayer, of our soul.

January 18

I dreamt last night of you,
It was so real, so true, I knew
You lived—although they said
You were dead.

I dreamt you kissed me, then
We laughed, just as we did when
You were here—before they said
That you were dead.

I know now you are alive.
I cannot see you but you are beside
Me still, as you were before they said—
So stupidly—that you were dead.

This was a dream I had of someone whom I loved very dearly and who was killed in the war. In my dream I cried, "But they said you were dead!" and he laughed.

January 19

Love in her sunny eyes does basking play;
Love walks the pleasant mazes of her hair;
Love does on both her lips for ever stray;
And sows and reaps a thousand kisses there.
In all her outward parts Love's always seen;
But, oh, he never went within.

A. COWLEY

In so many people who appear beautiful their characters and personalities are the opposite. Beauty to be compelling and memorable must come from the heart and soul.

19

January 20

Every day is a miracle. The world gets up in the morning and is fed and goes to work, and in the evening it comes home and is fed again and perhaps has a little amusement and goes to sleep. To make that possible, so much has to be done by so many people that, on the face of it, it is impossible. Well, every day we do it; and every day, come hell, or high water, we're going to have to go on doing it as well as we can.

JAMES GOULD COZZENS

If you think seriously of what this says, the world is a fantastic miracle, and if we are sensitive and intuitive we cannot take it all for granted.

January 21

We are bringing up a generation which is already suspicious and which will believe in nothing or nobody, unless we give them something by which they can sift the grain from the chaff, a way in which they can find the real truth amongst a tissue of lies.

There is a way to do this. It is the way we have done it ourselves, maybe unconsciously, but nevertheless unceasingly, all our lives. But, for us, the foundation-stone was there, given us by parents and grandparents, born in our blood and handed down through the centuries. It is an old way—a way that has never failed—it is called Faith.

January 22

Never undertake anything for which you wouldn't have the courage to ask the blessings of Heaven.

G. C. LICHTENBERG

January 23

It is a mistake to look too far ahead. Only one link in the chain of destiny can be handled at a time.

WINSTON CHURCHILL

I always try to remember this. One misses so many exciting and wonderful things today while wondering what will happen tomorrow or the day after.

January 24

I saw you look at me and knew
This was the moment I had sought,
And sought in vain—yes, it was true
That love could happen swift as thought,
I didn't know your name.

I saw your eyes look into mine,
My heart was beating, did you know?
We paused through centuries of time,
But there was nothing now to show
We'd loved in other lives.

Something flashed from me to you.
You were trembling, so was I.
We didn't speak and yet we knew
That everything we felt was true
Because we'd met again.

It is believed by some of those who seek the truth that we move in an octave with those we love or with those who mean something special in our lives. Therefore we meet and meet again, shuffled and reborn—but in a different guise. A husband may become a wife, a lover—a child, a brother—a father. But inevitably we remain still an indivisible and unbreakable part of each other.

January 25

A candle-flame is like tapering hands held palm to palm in prayer. It is a wavering yet hopeful fight against the darkness, a tiny, glowing reflection of the warmth of God.

I have lit candles in Catholic churches, tapers in Greek Orthodox ones, joss sticks in Indian and Chinese temples, and believe that as long as they burn, my prayer is heard in Heaven.

January 26

Shock takes people in strange ways. I've known women who have received news that the man they love best in the world has been killed put on their best dress and got out and dance. I've known older women roam the streets talking familiarly to any stranger who would listen, while unable to say one word to their nearest and dearest.

I have seen men break down and cry, and I've known others go out in a towering rage and try to kill the first man they meet. It is only those who have faith who turn to the only real source of help—God.

January 27

Love seeketh not itself to please,
Nor for itself hath any care,
But for another gives its ease,
And builds a Heaven in Hell's despair.

WILLIAM BLAKE

The love of a woman for a man, and a mother for her child, is shown in how she is prepared to give and sacrifice herself for them. But when a man is truly in love, his whole instinct is to care for and protect the woman to whom he has given his heart.

January 28

Lord, Thou knowest better than I know myself that I am growing older, and will some day be old. Keep me from the fatal habit of thinking that I must say something on every subject and on every occasion. Release me from craving to straighten out everybody's affairs.

Make me thoughtful but not moody, helpful but not bossy. With my vast store of wisdom, it seems a pity not to use it all—but Thou knowest, Lord, that I want a few friends at the end.

Keep my mind free from the recital of endless details . . . give me wings to get to the point. Seal my lips on aches and pains. They are increasing and love of rehearsing them is becoming sweeter as the years go by. I dare not ask for grace enough to enjoy the tales of others' pains, but help me to endure them with patience.

I dare not ask for improved memory, but for growing humility and a lessening cocksureness when my memory seems to clash with the memories of others. Teach me the glorious lesson that occasionally I may be mistaken.

Keep me reasonably sweet; I do want to be a saint . . . but not one who is hard to live with . . . for a sour old person is one of the crowning works of the devil. Give me the ability to see good things in unexpected places, and talents in unexpected people, and please give me the grace to tell them so.

Amen

This prayer I said first on my sixtieth birthday, and I have repeated it ever since. How easy to say, how difficult to do!

January 29

Cheer up! Remember today is the tomorrow you worried about yesterday.

Anon.

January 30

I dream a secret dream,
I search the sky and touch the sea,
I dream of mountains peaking high,
Of forests where no human's been,
And in my dream I search for thee.

I dream a secret dream
Of wild delight and love so sweet
That sunshine blinds my quivering eyes
And violets spring beneath my feet,
And in my dreams your lips I meet.

I dream a secret dream,
I hold a star against my breast,
I dream the moonbeams follow me
In tenderness, in tenderness,
And in my dreams I'm one with thee.

This is what every woman feels when she is in love, what every woman longs to feel and what every woman should feel sometime in her life.

January 31

All is not lost; th'unconquerable will,
And study of revenge, immortal hate
And courage never to submit or yield,
And what is else not to be overcome.

JOHN MILTON

On my Mother's gravestone I have written, "With courage never to submit or yield." It is what she had all her life. She suffered great financial difficulties. She lost her husband in the First World War and her two adored sons in 1940. But she said after Dunkirk:

"If crying would bring them back I would cry my eyes out, but I must just go on living to help other people."

That is courage.

February

February 1

Prayer is too often a request. Real prayer is the overwhelming desire to pray, to abandon everything in the desire to pierce the veil, to come near to the Godhead. But prayer, after all, is only thought. It is our thoughts which make us what we are. In the rush and hurry of civilized life we often find little time to think of the real things—the things that matter. How then should we have time to pray?

Prayer is essentially individual. Each person makes his own prayer and its form. It must meet our needs, but we determine the prayer itself as we determine the need for which we pray.

I once heard a little girl of five say:

"Please, dear God, keep me safe this night, and if there are creaks and squeaks in the dark, make me think it's only my tummy and not anything frightening!"

The Years of Opportunity

February 2

Small things are best:
Grief and unrest
To rank and wealth are given;
But little things
On little wings
Bear little souls to heaven.

F. W. FABER

A millionaire once showed me his treasures—pictures, furniture, jewels, all of great value. Then he opened a fine gold box and handed me what was inside.

"I have kept this all my life," he said. "I picked it the first time I walked on the moors in Scotland."

It was a piece of white heather.

February 3

If you're planning for one year, plant grain; if you're planning for ten years, plant trees, if you're planning for a hundred years, plant men.

OLD CHINESE PROVERB

February 4

As the sun shines down on dusty plain,
I think of a garden in the rain.
Of grey clouds drifting in from the sea,
To the misty land where I long to be.

The burning sky—a ball of fire,
The noise and the smell of the packed bazaar,
Creaking punkas bring no relief,
From the airless, suffocating heat.

I dream of lilacs in the Spring,
Of dew on the grass and birds which sing.
I see instead the barren sand,
Of this lonely, frightening, foreign land.

Once when I was in India, which I love dearly, I had a strange mystical experience. I picked up the misery and unhappiness of a woman who I knew had lived in the country, hated it and died there. I knew as clearly as if I could see her; she was small, red-headed, and came from Scotland. Her name was Annie.

February 5

Can it be seriously contemplated that all men's contributions are the same? It is variety and assortment in the qualities of men and nations that make the sum total of life. Respect and acknowledgement of each man's opportunity to add to his quota entail that tolerance and equal justice which are possible only in a democracy.

RONALD CARTLAND

February 6

A friend of my mother lost her two sons in 1917, her daughter had died as a little girl some years earlier. The poor woman was absolutely prostrate, feeling that her life was over, although she was comparatively young. She cried and cried, until the doctors called in by her husband said her mind was affected, and more or less gave up the case.

One night she was crying when suddenly she saw her two sons standing at the end of her bed, holding by the hand their small sister, and the eldest boy said:

"For goodness' sake, Mummy, pull yourself together. We're perfectly all right, but you're preventing us from getting on with what we have to do by all this weeping and wailing."

The children were clear, distinct, and looked just as they had in their lifetime. The mother had time to take in every detail of their appearance, then they were gone. From that day on she was a completely changed woman—cheerful and happy.

February 7

> Matthew, Mark, Luke and John,
> The bed be blessed that I lie on,
> Four angels to my bed,
> Four angels round my head
> One to watch, and one to pray
> And two to bear my soul away.
>
> **THOMAS ADY**

This old prayer, written in 1655, often lingers in my mind. I had my whole house blessed in every room before I moved into it, and the atmosphere is therefore one of peace and happiness, and the angels round my bed protect me when I sleep.

February 8

Men are wonderful, but so many women are afraid to admit it in case it detracts something from them. But a man one loves is part of oneself and to make him wonderful, we too must be wonderful in thought, word, deed and, of course, heart.

February 9

> Lord, make me an instrument of Your peace,
> Where there is hatred, let me sow love;
> Where there is injury, pardon;
> Where there is doubt, faith;
> Where there is despair, hope;
> Where there is darkness, light;

And where there is sadness, joy.
O divine Master, grant that I may not
So much seek to be consoled as to console;
To be understood as to understand;
To be loved as to love;
For it is in giving that we receive;
It is in pardoning that we are pardoned;
And it is in dying
That we are born to eternal life.

Amen

SAINT FRANCIS OF ASSISI

To so many of the unhappy and despairing, Saint Francis has been a life-line, and all of us learn sooner or later "it is in giving that we receive."

February 10

A man should never be ashamed to own he has been in the wrong, which is but saying, in other words, that he is wiser today than he was yesterday.

JONATHAN SWIFT

How hard it is to remember this, how hard to make one's tongue say: "I am sorry I was wrong, and you were right." I pray to be big enough to admit my faults, not to God—He knows them already—but to men—and women!

February 11

God be in my head,
And in my understanding;

God be in my eyes,
And in my looking;

God be in my mouth,
And in my speaking;

God be in my heart,
And in my thinking;

God be at my end,
And at my departing.

SARUM MISSAL

*This is the perfect all-embracing prayer for every day, every year,
every life.*

February 12

*Mohammed made the people believe he would call a hill to him and
from the top of it offer up his prayers for the observers of his law. The
people assembled: Mohammed called the hill to come to him again and
again; and when the hill stood still, he was not in the least abashed,
but said: "If the hill will not come to Mohammed, Mohammed will go
to the hill."*

*How wise he was. So often in life we have to make the generous
gesture. It does not humiliate, but enlarges and enriches our characters
and personalities.*

February 13

For this is Wisdom; to love, to live,
To take what Fate, or the gods, may give.
L. ADAMS BECK, *The Garden of Karma*

February 14

Bring me my bow of burning gold!
Bring me my arrows of desire!
Bring me my spear! O clouds unfold!
Bring me my chariot of fire.
I will not cease from mortal fight,
Nor shall my sword sleep in my hand
Till we have built Jerusalem
In England's green and pleasant land.
WILLIAM BLAKE

This rouses my whole being and every time I hear it I pledge myself anew. On the memorial of my brother Ronald I have inscribed "I will not cease from mental fight" and I know he never will.

February 15

A jest or a laughing word often describes the highest matters better than sharpness and genius.
HORACE

Horace was a man who enjoyed life. How right he was about many things but in this he was very wise. In laughter can often be heard the voice of God.

February 16

How do I love thee? Let me count the ways,
I love thee to the depth and breadth and height
My soul can reach, when feeling out of sight
For the ends of Being and ideal Grace.

ELIZABETH BARRETT BROWNING

*This in four lines is the perfect story of love. For our souls, or if we
prefer, our hearts, are limited by themselves. Yet love gives us new
breadth and height and new horizons.*

February 17

I live alone, dear Lord,
    Stay by my side,
In all my daily needs
    Be Thou my guide.
Grant my good health,
    For that indeed I pray.
To carry on my work
    From day to day.
Keep pure my mind,
    My thoughts, my every deed.
Let me be kind, unselfish
    In my neighbour's need.
Spare me from fire,
    From flood, malicious tongues;
From thieves;
    From fear and evil ones.

If sickness
   Or an accident befall,
Then humbly, Lord, I pray
   Hear thou my call.
And when I'm feeling low,
   Or in despair,
Lift up my heart
   And help me in my prayer.
I live alone, dear Lord,
   Yet have no fear
Because I feel
   Your presence ever near.

                                        Amen

This is a prayer I was given in the magnificent Cathedral in Mexico City. I feel it will help many people who feel lonely and find it hard to remember they are, in fact, never alone.

February 18

There are many faiths, but the spirit is one, in me, in you, and in every man.

LEO TOLSTOY

February 19

The story of the Battle of Britain I can never forget is of Mr. Churchill going to the Headquarters of Air Vice-Marshal K. R. Parks, who was commanding the all-important No. 11 Group. On the radar screen the Prime Minister watched the advance of the German bombers. As each wave approached, the Air Vice-Marshal gave his orders to put in to the British fighter squadrons.

Calm, quiet and authoritative, the Air Marshal's voice showed no sign of emotion, and Mr. Churchill, tense, his bulldog face set, watched in silence. Each attack was successfully repelled, but to the waves of German bombers there seemed to be no end. Wave after wave appeared, wave upon wave . . . .

At last Mr. Churchill turned abruptly. "How many more have you got?"

The Air Marshal's voice didn't alter. "I am putting in my last."

Their eyes fixed on the screen, the two men waited for the next German wave. It never came. With tears in his eyes Winston Churchill got into his car. It was on his way back to London that he composed the immortal phrase: "Never in the field of human conflict has so much been owed by so many to so few."

February 20

When God formed the rose He said, "Thou shalt flourish and spread thy perfume." When He commanded the sun to emerge from chaos, He added, "Thou shalt enlighten and warm the world." When he gave his life to the lark, He enjoined upon it to soar and sing in the air. Finally He created man, and told him to love. And seeing the sun shine, perceiving the rose scattering its odours, hearing the lark warble in the air, how can man help loving?

ANASTASIUS GRÜN

February 21

Above all, we cannot afford not to live in the present. He is blessed over all mortals who loses no moment of the passing life in remembering the past.

HENRY DAVID THOREAU

Live today fully, this is the message, and the only things I regret in my life are those I didn't do, not the ones I did.

February 22

Little boy kneels at the foot of the bed,
Droops on the little hands little gold head.
Hush! Hush! Whisper who dares!
Christopher Robin is saying his prayers.

A. A. MILNE

What mother has not read this with a tear in her eye? All too soon our children grow up, and the moment when we watched them pray has passed. But because we taught them their prayers we have given them something on which they can rely, which will help them in danger and preserve them from evil all through their lives.

February 23

Taoism is acting without design, occupying yourself without making a business of it, finding the great in what is small and the many in the few, repaying injury with kindness, effecting difficult things while they are easy, and managing great things in their beginnings; this is the method of the Tao.

LAO-TSE

February 24

Many waters cannot quench love, neither can the floods drown it: if a man would give all the substance of his house for love, it would utterly be condemned . . . .

The Song of Solomon

February 25

The splendour of Greece still lights our skies, reaching over America and Asia and lands which the Greeks never dreamed existed. There would be no Christianity as we know it without the fertilizing influence of the Greek Fathers of the Church, who owed their training to Greek philosophy.

By a strange accident all the images of Buddha in the Far East can be traced back to portraits of Alexander, who seemed to Greeks to be Apollo incarnate.

We owe to the Greeks the beginning of science and the beginning of thought. They built the loveliest temples ever made, carved marble with delicacy and strength, and set in motion the questing mind which refuses to believe there are any bounds to reason.

ROBERT PAYNE, *The Splendour of Greece*

February 26

Winston Churchill described in The World Crisis *how, when in 1914 he was asked to become First Lord of the Admiralty, he opened the Bible at random and found encouragement and reassurance from the verses on which his eyes fell.*

I often open the Bible in the same way for guidance on a difficult problem. Sometimes it has no obvious answer for me, but once in a desperately difficult situation which would have far-reaching consequences, but not only on me but on my family, my finger touched a verse which was very clearly the reply to my question.

February 27

How ungrateful we are! I often think of the story of the Saint who promised to try to grant the desires of all those who sought his help. For two days there was a great crowd outside the cave where he lived. On the third day he came out to find only one person outside, a small ragged boy.

"Where have all the people gone, my son?" the Saint asked.

"Home," replied the boy, pointing to the village far away on the horizon. "You have given them all they wanted."

"And you?"

"I came to offer thanks, Holy Father, for you cured me of a grievous itch."

"And of all those I helped you are the only one to return and give thanks?"

"Yes, Father, but who knows . . . I might get it again!"

February 28

There is an Indian parable which illustrates the value of the infinitely little. A prisoner in a great tower directs his wife to bring to its foot a beetle, a silk thread, and a little honey. She is to attach the silk to the beetle, to smear his horns with honey, and set him free to climb the tower, following the scent of the honey. He does it. A twine is attached to the silk thread, a rope to the twine and the prisoner is freed. The infinitely little has conquered.

L. ADAMS BECK, The Way of Power

February 29

I see my way as birds their trackless way,
I shall arrive! what time, what circuit first,
I ask not: but unless God send His hail
Or blinding fireballs, sleet or stifling snow,
In some time, His good time, I shall arrive:
He guides me and the bird. In His good time!

PARACELSUS

How impatient we often are for the things we have asked of God, and yet in His own time, in His own way, He never fails us. If we trust Him, then we would save ourselves so many hours and days of worry and unhappiness.

March

March 1

One day in a small village in Bengal, an ascetic woman from the neighbourhood came to see me. She had the name Sarvakhepi given to her by the village people, the meaning of which is "the woman who is mad about all things."

She fixed her star-like eyes upon my face and startled me with the question "When are you coming to meet me underneath the trees?" Evidently she pitied me who lived (according to her) prisoned behind walls, banished away from the great meeting-place of the All, where she had her dwelling.

Just at that moment my gardener came with his basket, and when the woman understood that the flowers in the vase on my table were going to be thrown away, to make place for the fresh ones, she looked pained and said to me, "You are always engaged reading and writing, you do not see."

Then she took the discarded flowers in her palms, kissed them and touched them with her forehead, and reverently murmured to herself, "Beloved of my heart."

I felt that this woman, in her direct vision of the infinite personality in the heart of all things, truly represented the spirit of India.

RABINDRANATH TAGORE

March 2

I say no man has ever yet been half
                devout enough,
None has ever yet adored or worship'd
                half enough,
None has begun to think how divine he
                himself is, and
how certain the future is.

WALT WHITMAN

March 3

And yet I wish but for the thing I have:
My bounty is as boundless as the sea,
My love as deep; the more I give to thee,
The more I have, for both are infinite.

Romeo and Juliet

We so often forget that love is boundless and we don't have to divide it into portions. The more we give, the more there is to give and the nearer we get to God.

March 4

Oh, Thou who art! Ecclesiastes names thee the Almighty; Maccabees names thee Creator; the Epistle to the Ephesians names thee Liberty; Baruch names thee Immensity; the

Psalms name thee Wisdom and Truth; John names thee Light; the Book of Kings names thee Lord; Exodus calls thee Providence; Leviticus, Holiness; Esdras, Justice; Creation calls thee God; Man names thee Father; but Solomon names thee Compassion, and that is the most beautiful of all thy names.

VICTOR HUGO

Compassion to me means the desire to change the conditions of the person for whom I am sorry. I always feel the Good Samaritan should have fought to get back for the man he befriended what had been stolen.

March 5

A woman must seek all her life until she finds in one man the complete, perfect love which is both human and divine. Any sacrifice is worthwhile when one knows the ecstasy, the glory and the irresistible fires of love.

March 6

Creatures, plants, horses, cows, men, elephants, whatsoever breathes, whether moving or flying and, in addition, whatsoever is immovable—all this is led by mind and is supported on mind. Mind is the final reality.

Indian Scripture

March 7

> *"The year's at the spring,*
> *And day's at the morn;*
> *Morning's at seven;*
> *The hill-side's dew-pearled;*
> *The lark's on the wing;*
> *The snail's on the thorn:*
> *God's in his heaven -*
> *All's right with the world!"*

ROBERT BROWNING

I feel like singing this when I see the first snowdrop, the first green bud, the first baby chick. Spring is a message of hope, so exquisite, so perfect that we often forget it is God's message to man that life is eternal. There is no darkness, no death—only light and life!

March 8

By swallowing evil words unsaid no one has ever yet harmed his stomach.

WINSTON CHURCHILL

It is hard to bite back bitter or angry words when we are hurt, but we can save ourselves so much more misery by not fighting back, by not giving the person who has insulted us "a piece of mind."

March 9

My brother Ronald said that so many people try to put prayer into a straitjacket. It must be elastic and dynamic. Prayer has many aspects—the gabbled formula of those who say, "I always say the prayers I learnt as a child," the physical and mental effect of spiritual striving—Jesus in the Garden of Gethsemane; contemplation—a few minutes in an empty church; meditation—for those who can concentrate to the exclusion of worldly things; gratitude—thanks and praise, the most often forgotten of all the categories of prayer.

March 10

Behold, I stand at the door, and knock: if any man hear my voice, and open the door, I will come in to him, and will sup with him, and he with me.

Revelation

We often forget that we have been told over and over again to ask God for everything we want. But we also forget to listen to His answer.

March 11

Courage is not freedom from fear; it is being afraid and going on.

Anon.

Courage is the most important of all emotions because it brings out the best in us, it makes us face the truth, and more than anything else it invigorates and inspires.

When we pray we should say: "Lord, let me never be defeated, help me never to give up, as You Yourself never cease fighting for us."

March 12

> Do all the good you can,
> By all the means you can
> In all the ways you can,
> At all the turns you can,
> To all the people you can,
> As long as ever you can.
>
> JOHN WESLEY

March 13

Nothing is so beautiful as a child going to sleep while he is saying his prayers, says God.
I tell you nothing is so beautiful in the world . . . .

CHARLES PÉGUY

We who are older learnt our first prayers from our mothers. Today many children hear prayers only from strangers. A child's prayers give him a sense of security with God and also with his mother and his home.

March 14

Love is a flame which burns in heaven, and whose soft reflections radiate to us; two worlds are opened, two lives given to it; it is by love that we double our being; it is by love that we approach God.

AIMÉ-MARTIN

March 15

To love or not we are no more free
Than a ripple to rise and leave the sea.
The Garden of Karma

March 16

The light was the strange light of dawn. There were numbers of birds already, little ones that sang praises madly in the hedges and big ones that moved in long lines against the golden east, flying from north to south in slow rhythmical ecstasy. Some of them were black and some were white.

"Crows and gulls," said Lucilla, "and they fly like that because they are so happy that the sun has risen. They can't sing like the little birds and so they have to praise God with the movement of their wings."

"What an awful thing it would be," said David, "if suddenly one morning God forgot to tell the sun to get up."

"I think that's what the birds feel," said Lucilla. "They do get so excited, don't they, when they find it's all right and He hasn't forgotten."

"Could he ever forget?" asked David anxiously.

"Of course not," Lucilla replied. "He always remembers everything."

"How clever He is," said David.

ELIZABETH GOUDGE, *The Bird in the Tree*

March 17

Tradition and patriotism are a call to man's higher feelings, to something beyond his own immediate self. Love of country breeds service.

RONALD CARTLAND

March 18

Let not one look of fortune cast you down;
She were not fortune, if she did not frown:
Such as do braveliest bear her scorn awhile,
Are those on whom, at last, she most will smile.

JOHN BOYLE, EARL OF CORK AND ORRERY

Life for all of us is filled with ups and downs, but that is what makes it an adventure. Without the struggle there would not be joy and glory of survival.

March 19

I always love to begin a journey on Sundays because I shall have the prayer of the Church, to preserve all that travel by land or by water.

JONATHAN SWIFT

March 20

Grant yourself a moment of peace and you will understand how foolishly you have scurried about.

Learn how to be silent and you will notice that you have talked much too much.

Be kind and you will realize that your judgement of others was too severe.

TSCHEN TSCHI JU

March 21

The day returns and brings us the petty round of irritating concerns and duties. Help us to play the man, help us to perform them with laughter and kind faces; let cheerfulness abound with industry. Give us to go blithely on our business all this day, bring us to our resting beds weary and content and undishonoured, and grant us in the end the gift of sleep.

ROBERT LOUIS STEVENSON

March 22

The truest end of Life is to know that Life never
  ends . . . .
For tho' Death be a Dark Passage, it leads to Immortality,
And that's Recompense enough for suffering of it.

WILLIAM PENN

March 23

When you wish upon a star,
As all lovers must,
Wish that the wonder of this hour
Will never turn to dust.

I feel the beating of your heart,
The ecstasy and thrill,
You will be of me a part,
Until the sun stands still.

Love can never be lost, once given it becomes ours and we can hold it for eternity.

March 24

Did you suffer in an alien land?
Did you weep at being far from Rome?
Did the conqueror's foot on miles of sand
Mean anything except it was not home?

The Romans won and lost the world,
The Greeks, the Goths, the French all fought
For power, while holy Spain unfurled
Horrors and cruelty of another sort.

So many broken lives, so many tears,
What does it mean in centuries to come?
Can broken pillars tell us of the fears
That women feel, while men still beat the drum?

Standing in the ruins of Dougga in Tunisia which had been a flourishing city when the Romans conquered North Africa, I wondered if the power and glory of victors can ever justify the heartbreak of the women who, torn from their homes and all that is familiar, suffer agonies of anxiety while their men make war.

March 25

And say not thou that former years were better than those of the present time; for that is the talk of a foolish person.

ECCLESIASTICUS

As we grow old we are all inclined to talk about "the good old days," but today will become the past, then we will be saying how good things were.

How much more sensible to enjoy every moment of the present, and to find it delightful, exciting, and perhaps a challenge.

March 26

In this brief life the memory of one hour
Of perfect love is worth all the joys,
And he who has it not, though he be king,
Goes beggared through the world.

ELLA WHEELER WILCOX

March 27

Heaped fruit, vegetables and grain,
Mustard, marsala, musk and ghee.
Dust rising in clouds to fall again
On silk and silver, gold and tea.
Crowds drifting, jostling, wandering where?
With Brahmini bulls, sacred and old.
Veiled women giggling stop and stare,
Or listen to the storyteller's ode.
This is India under a burning sun,
The glory of the dawn o'er plain and peak.
Swift opal twilight when the day is done,
And nights of whispered magic as men speak
Of gods and love, rebellion, battles won.
Here hides the truth for which I seek.

How I love India, the Red Fort at Delhi, the pink splendour of Jaipur, the unbelievable ethereal beauty of the Taj Mahal and the unquenchable faith radiating from the pilgrims bathing in the Ganges at Benares! India gives to everyone who visits her something spiritual to take away.

March 28

Kindness can charm a snake from its hole.

FIRDAUSI

March 29

Through Love all things become lighter which understanding thought too heavy.

HATIF

March 30

For the Greeks the whole world was a divine field, and men were only a little less than gods. The Greeks knew that without the knowledge of the divine presence life loses its savour, falls into the artifices of corruption and turns into nightmare. They remained faithful to their gods because to do otherwise was to lose faith with themselves.

When Saint Paul declared: "Where no law is, there is no transgression," he was proclaiming a universal truth well known to the Greeks: unless we live under a divine law, then all crimes are permitted to us, and all art is meaningless, and all purposes are vain.

The Splendour of Greece

March 31

O lead my spirit:
O raise it from these heavy depths, transported by Thy Art that fearlessly and joyfully it soar up to Thee. For Thou, Thou knowest all things, Thou alone canst inspire.

BEETHOVEN

April

April 1

Glory be to God for dappled things—
    For skies of couple-colour as a brinded cow;
      For rose-moles all in stipple upon trout that swim;
Fresh-firecoal chestnut-falls; finches' wings;
    Landscape plotted and pieced—gold, fallow, and
plough;
      And all trades, their gear and tackle and trim.

All things counter, original, spare, strange;
    Whatever is fickle, freckled (who knows how?)
    With swift, slow; sweet, sour; adazzle, dim;
He fathers-forth whose beauty is past change:
    Praise Him.

GERARD MANLEY HOPKINS

April 2

"O God, who sent Your servant, Saint John the Baptist, to be a voice crying in the wilderness to prepare the way for the coming of Christ. Through the intercession of Saint John, under whose Cross we sail, save us now in our extremity and, if we cannot be saved, then let us die with the courage that the Knights of the Order have shown all down the centuries."

I wrote this prayer for my novel The Dream and the Glory, *which is sold for the St. John Ambulance Brigade. There is to me nothing more wonderful and inspiring than the great ideal and selfless devotion of those who give their time and their lives to "the Service of Mankind."*

When you see the Ambulance and Nursing members in their black-and-white uniforms at First Aid posts, at sports rallies, at football matches, protest marches, riots and public demonstrations, will you remember they are unpaid and unthanked, and yet their dedication is in itself a prayer to God?

April 3

And what is prayer? So few people seem to know the uplifting of the spirit, the linking-up with something vital, splendid and forceful outside ourselves and yet of which we are a part; or that spiritual striving which sometimes results in a miraculous and inner peace, but which is not and never can be a morning and evening exercise.

April 4

Teach us, good Lord,
To serve Thee as Thou deservest,
To give and not to count the cost,
To fight and not to heed the wounds,
To toil and not to seek for rest,
To labour and not to ask for any reward,
Save that of knowing that we do Thy will.

IGNATIUS OF LOYOLA

April 5

Youth is happy because it has the ability to see beauty. Anyone who keeps the ability to see beauty never grows old.

FRANZ KAFKA

How much beauty there is around us: we should mirror it in ourselves so we too become beautiful.

A shaft of sunshine to light the eyes, the song of the birds to bring music to the voice. Even in a crowded city there is the beauty of the sky above us.

April 6

There is so much good in the worst of us,
And so much bad in the best of us,
That it hardly becomes any of us
To talk about the rest of us.

E. W. HOCH

How dull the world would be if we never gossiped! But there is gossip and gossip! I have seen such unhappiness caused by those who have repeated what is cruel and unkind and, often, completely untrue.

Kings in the olden days cut off the heads of messengers who brought them bad news. I refuse to listen when people begin to say to me. "I think you ought to know . . . ." I am quite sure it is something I do not wish to hear.

We laugh and talk about ourselves and our friends, but we should always leave behind a note of hope and encouragement.

April 7

Four ducks on a pond,
A grassy bank beyond,
A blue sky of spring,
White clouds on the wing;
What a little thing
To remember for years—
To remember with tears!

WILLIAM ALLINGHAM

As one gets older it is the little things one remembers and the little things which tug at our heart-strings.

April 8

It was that moment of approaching sunset when the flaming patches of gorse, the wild marsh flowers, the sea-grasses, the crimson, peaty earth, the creeks and gullies of blue water were yielding to the last demands of the sun all that they possessed of glory. The line of the distant sea was jade-green, the sky turquoise.

ELIZABETH GOUDGE, *The Herbs of Grace*

April 9

How much impression do we make on the places where we live? Who will deny that homes have atmosphere, even as people have personalities? Perhaps what we call atmosphere is a mixture of personality, character, and emotion accumulated down the centuries, each owner contributing his quota until the house itself becomes a transmitter vibrating to the life force it secretes. And can we not understand all too plainly that a house which has been in a family for many generations becomes part of the family itself?

What stirs within my restless heart,
What magic trembles and awakes,
Like ripples from a wind-stirred harp
In this remote enchanted place?

Haunting! Taunting, sweet wild singing
Flash of silver leaping flame.
Phantoms mist-blown magic winging
Calling me again . . . again.

April 10

Bid me to live, and I will live,
  Thy Protestant to be:
Or bid me love, and I will give
  A loving heart to thee,
A heart as soft, a heart as kind,
  A heart as sound and free
As in the whole world thou canst find,
  That heart I'll give to thee.

ROBERT HERRICK

This is an expression of love as Robert Herrick felt it over three hundred years ago, but today every man feels the same when he finds the woman he really loves.

April 11

Dear God, even when we do not need the sun, there is still the moon and the stars and the lamp on a winter's evening—there is so much beautiful light in the world.

WILHELM RAABE

Light is the greatest gift of God and with it the power to see it not only with our eyes, but with our souls. The Greeks depicted rays of light coming from the solar plexus. The Christians put these rays on the heads of their saints and called it a halo.

April 12

> So many gods, so many creeds,
>> So many paths that wind and wind,
> While just the art of being kind
>> Is all the sad world needs.
>
> ELLA WHEELER WILCOX

What is so wonderful is that all creeds and gods lift our minds and our souls upward, to everything that is best and finest within ourselves!

God has given us free will to be elated, aroused ecstatically and encouraged by what suits us best. But eventually, by whatever path we travel, our pilgrimage ends with Him. So we are never alone or lonely. He is always there to guide us forwards and upwards.

April 13

There is, after all, no such thing as security in this world. The only resource for the soul of man is the cheerful acceptance of insecurity: steeling the spirit to bear whatever happens. Nothing will take the place of inner fortitude.

DAVID GRAYSON

April 14

> Deep peace of the Running Wave to you.
> Deep peace of the Flowing Air to you.
> Deep peace of the Quiet Earth to you.
> Deep peace of the Shining Stars to you.
> Deep peace of the Son of Peace to you.
>
> *Celtic Benediction*

April 15

I want—I stretch out hungry hands
To dreams which always evade my touch.
And treasures of wisdom from ancient lands
Are lost because I ask too much.

Did I ever know the mystic truth
Which sometimes a word will help recall?
Bitterly in my soul's sweet youth
I've learnt that idols fall.

I want—the blue-grey mountain mists,
The shadowy darkness of forest trees.
The rough waves by the moonbeams kissed
Hurt me—like falling leaves.

I wrote this when I was twenty-one, full of yearning for something beyond the commonplace and the ordinary—something spiritual I could not grasp.

April 16

We said good-bye in the pouring rain,
I didn't cry, it was too much pain
To speak.

"Good-bye." What a hopeless word it seemed,
When everything of which we'd dreamed
Had gone.

Yet if we lived it all again,
I'd still endure that deadly pain
For love.

Hasn't everyone a moment of pain in their life, when because they love they suffer agonizingly? And yet who would refuse the wonder, joy and agony of love?

April 17

Little deeds of kindness, little words of love,
Help to make earth happy, like to heaven above.

JULIA CARNEY

How often we forget the little words of thanks, of praise, or encouragement. When we look back at our own life we remember not the gifts we have been given, but the smile, the kiss, the praise which have helped and enriched us. We must pray not to forget to give freely these "little things" to everyone we meet today.

April 18

Don't commiserate with your fellow man. Help him.

MAXIM GORKY

April 19

Talk happiness. The world is sad enough
Without your woe. No path is wholly rough.
Look for the places that are smooth and clear,
And speak of them to rest the weary ear
Of earth; so hurt by one continuous strain
Of mortal discontent and grief and pain.

Talk faith. The world is better off without
Your uttered ignorance and morbid doubt.
If you have faith in God, or man, or self,
Say so; if not, push back upon the shelf
Of silence all your thoughts till faith shall come.
No one will grieve because your lips are dumb.

Talk health. The dreary, never-ending tale
of mortal maladies is worn and stale;
You cannot charm or interest or please
By harping on that minor chord disease.
Say you are well, or all is well with you,
And God shall hear your words and make them true.

ELLA WHEELER WILCOX

April 20

Tiptoe away and close the Gates,
The Gates of Dreams Come True;
Your chariot, Common Sense, awaits,
To the world it must carry you.
Back again, perhaps you will say:
"How silly was I to think
That Kindliness was the Golden Way,
And Love 'the Missing Link.'"
Forget if you will, for a little while,
Let the "grown-up" part of you
Scoff with a surpercilious smile
At the thought of Dreams Come True.
But when the moon is very bright,
And darkness hides the day,
You will see the sails of night
Unfurl a familiar way . . . .

Happiness is in the mind. When you are tired, ill or miserable, try making a picture of beauty and tell yourself a story of love. If you do it frequently you will find yourself both happier and lovelier in body and soul.

April 21

The Greeks and Romans both believed in the healing power of dreams, and in ancient Rome the College of the Inspired Dreams was a place of gathering for those who were sick or sad.

It was dedicated to Asclepius the Healer, and it was believed he was the inspirer of these dreams. Those needing help slept in the quiet of the sacred cloisters and seldom without result.

One sees exactly why that should be and wishes such help could be given now, and without human intervention, to those who need it. But it is a true saying that we can participate in heaven and its gifts only in so far as heaven is within ourselves.

The Splendour of Greece

April 22

Not in the Utopia—subterranean fields—
Or some secreted island, Heaven knows where!
But in the very world, which is the world
Of all of us—the place where in the end
We find our happiness, or not at all.

WILLIAM WORDSWORTH

April 23

My brother Ronald always prayed before he made a speech; so do I. It is incidentally the best panacea for nerves. I pray that something I say may help just one person who is listening. I pray that I shall speak the truth, and that it shall be the truth, not only my point of view.

April 24

> I sit beside my lonely fire,
>   And pray for wisdom yet,
> For calmness to remember
>   Or courage to forget.
>
> CHARLES H. AIDÉ

We all wish for wisdom, but it is rare to find people who really try to forget. Far too many look back and regret.

I try never to do this. What is past is past and I believe it is the present and the future that count. There is in all of us the divine hope which makes us believe that there is always a new horizon and a new day when the sun will rise glorious and golden.

April 25

The English are not anything like so disagreeable at home as they are in travelling.

W. D. HOWELLS

People are disagreeable when they are travelling because they are frightened. They worry about themselves, their luggage, and their destination! Airplanes and trains are noisy monsters. Always start a journey like I do, carry with you a talisman which you believe will keep you safe.

I have a small diamond cross which has travelled over 500,000 miles on my wrist and in my handbag a medallion from Notre Dame de Laghet, who has saved thousands of people from accidents.

April 26

A kind word, a kind action, even a smile when it is needed, in my experience is rewarded a thousandfold. But equally we pay the penalty of unkindness and indifference. I often say to my children:
  "Nothing is for free in this world, and we reap what we sow."

April 27

I beseech you, in the bowels of Christ, think it possible you may be mistaken.

OLIVER CROMWELL

We are often mistaken even when we are convinced we are right. If we are, then we must, for the good of our souls, say so and apologize.

April 28

LORD,
Quiet the storms!
Be still, my soul, that the
divine may work in you.

We have found often enough
that the world can give
us no peace. Let us experience
the truth of the promise that
nothing in the world can take
from us Your Peace.

KIERKEGAARD

April 29

Lukewarmness I account a sin,
As great in love as in religion.
ABRAHAM COWLEY

*The lukewarm, the unenthusiastic, the people who say "I don't know"
to everything are a cross we all have to bear. They sap our vitality by
their very ineffectiveness, but it is still our duty to try to galvanize
them into life.*

April 30

It was because it was so full of white wings that Fairhaven
was such a happy place; wings of the yachts, of the seagulls,
and of the swans who divided their time between the Abbey
river, several miles to the eastward, and the blue lake in the
marsh where the sea-lavender grew. White wings are for ever
happy, symbols of escape and ascent, of peace and joy, and a
spot of earth about which they beat is secure of its happiness.
ELIZABETH GOUDGE, *The Bird in the Tree*

May

May 1

Would that the little Flowers were born to live,
Conscious of half the pleasure which they give;
That to this mountain daisy's self were known
The beauty of its star-shaped shadow, thrown
On the smooth surface of this naked stone!

WILLIAM WORDSWORTH

Flowers are thoughts of love, and of kindness,
Flowers help when we are unhappy, or sick:
Flowers celebrate anniversaries,
Flowers bring back memories.
Flowers are sent when we come into the world,
Flowers are given when we leave it,
Flowers will I know fill Heaven, for
Flowers reflect the beauty of God.

May 2

Who among us can say that the war did not bring its moments of wonder and glory? Moments when we knew that we were not alone—now or ever.

A friend of mine who was buried underneath her own house for five hours told of her experiences.

"At first I was just numb from the shock," she said. "I felt nothing except a dazed surprise that I was not in pain. Then my legs, which were prisoned beneath a beam, began to hurt, and I was afraid, desperately, horribly afraid . . . I think I screamed. I know that I was frantic to get free. Time passed. I felt choked by the dust. I thought I might be dying.

"I think I drifted into a semi-consciousness. But suddenly my brain seemed to clear and I knew that it was all unimportant. It didn't matter—the shattered house, my imprisoned body—I was still there. I myself and alive, with a new sort of inward aliveness I can't explain. It seems ridiculous to say it, but I was happy—happier than I've ever been in my life before. I had no vision, no visitation from another world, but I was not alone. I can't put it into words. I only know I would give everything I possess in the world to experience again that feeling of surety and completeness."

May 3

She is Language; he is Thought
She is Prudence; he is Law.
He is Reason; she is Sense.
She is Duty; he is Right.
He is Will; she is Wish.
He is Pity; she is Gift.
He is Song; she is Note.

She is Fuel; he is Fire.
She is Glory; He is Sun.
She is Motion; he is Wind.
He is Owner; she is Wealth.
He is Battle; she is Might.
He is Lamp; she is Light.
He is Day; she is Night.
He is Justice; she is Pity.
He is Channel; she is River.
She is Beauty; he is Strength.
She is Body; he is Soul.

VISHNU PURANA (LEGEND) - *"The Union of Man
and Woman"*

May 4

Love rules the court, the camp, the grove,
And men below, and saints above;
For love is Heaven, and Heaven is Love.

SIR WALTER SCOTT

May 5

*We all need courage to forget slights, snubs, unkindness, but as we
grow older they fade from our memories and most of all we gain the
wisdom to know that they were really of no consequence because they
could not hurt our souls.*

May 6

There is only one task, and that is to increase the store of love within us.

LEO TOLSTOY

May 7

In the name of the Father, the Son, and the Holy
  Ghost,
Blessed be the Holy and Immaculate Conception
  of the Blessed Virgin Mary, Mother of God.
Our Lady of Lourdes, pray for us.
Our Mother, have pity on us.
Our Lady of Lourdes, heal us, for the love and
  honour of the Blessed Trinity.
Our Lady of Lourdes, heal us, for the conversion
  of sinners.
Health of the sick, pray for us.
O Mary, conceived without sin, pray for us who
  have recourse to thee.

O God, who through the Immaculate Conception of the Blessed Virgin Mary, didst prepare a fit dwelling for Thy Son, grant us, we beseech Thee, who celebrate the Apparition of this Immaculate Virgin, health of soul and body. Through the same Jesus Christ, our Lord.

Amen

This prayer comes from the beautiful shrine at Lourdes, where so many sick and crippled have been cured. I say this prayer when I am ill and I know it is heard.

May 8

Who reproves the lame must go upright.

SAMUEL DANIEL

I like this variation of "people in glass houses shouldn't throw stones"!

May 9

Ships that pass in the night, and speak
    each other in passing;
Only a signal shown and a distant voice in
    the darkness;
So on the ocean of life we pass and speak
    one another,
Only a look and a voice; then darkness again
    and a silence.

HENRY W. LONGFELLOW

Ships which pass in the night yet sometimes linger. I know nothing more exciting than to know as my eyes meet those belonging to a stranger, that a magnetic spark unites us. Have we met before in previous lives? Have we some strange affinity which cannot be explained? "A look and a voice" and sometimes, God willing, more.

May 10

If I can do some good today,
If I can serve along life's way,
If I can something helpful say,
Lord, show me how.

GRENVILLE KLEISER

May 11

Love much. Earth has enough of bitter in it.
Cast sweets into its cup whene'er you can.
No heart so hard, but love at last may win it.
Love is the grand primaeval cause of man.
All hate is foreign to the first great plan.

Love much. There is no waste in freely giving;
More blessed is it, even, than to receive.
He who loves much alone finds life worth living;
Love on, through doubt and darkness, and believe
There is no thing which Love may not achieve.

ELLA WHEELER WILCOX

May 12

When I am dying, lean over me tenderly, softly,
    Stoop, as the yellow roses droop in the wind from
the south
So I may when I wake, if there be an Awakening,
    Keep, what lulled me to sleep, the touch of your
lips on my mouth.

The Garden of Karma

May 13

There's a long, long trail a-winding
Into the land of my dreams,
Where the nightingales are singing
And a white moon beams:
There's a long, long night of waiting
Until my dreams all come true;
Till the day when I'll be going down
That long, long trail with you.

STODDARD KING

When I was young I used to hear the soldiers singing this song as they went off to the mud and blood of the trenches in Flanders. So few returned, so many died.

But in those familiar words there is the note of unquestionable hope which keeps men sane in a strange hell of destruction and which keeps them idealistic, despite the misery and degradation of war.

May 14

I love thee with a love I seemed to lose
With my lost saints—I love thee with the breath,
Smiles, tears of all my life! and, if God choose,
I shall but love thee better after death.

ELIZABETH BARRETT BROWNING

We never lose love because love is God. Love from someone who is the other half of ourselves transcends the difficulties of life and every barrier of death. Pray today that you may find that love.

May 15

The story is told that when Apollo left the holy island of Delos to conquer Greece, a dolphin guided his ship to the little town of Crisa beneath the Shining Cliffs. The young god leaped from the ship disguised as a star at high noon; flames soared from him and the flash of splendour lit the sky; and then the star vanished, and there was only a young man armed with a bow and arrows.

He marched up the steep road to the lair of the dragon, who guarded the cliffs, and when the dragon was slain, he announced in a clear, ringing voice to all the gods that he claimed possession of all the territory he could see from where he was standing. He was among other things the god of good taste, and he had chosen the loveliest view in Greece.

It is a haunting view, and no one has quite succeeded in explaining why the view is so intensely satisfying. There is the faint blue sea in the distance and a valley of grey-blue olive-trees below and blue mountains curving away to left and right, and the Shining Cliffs rise protectively behind; and there is a kind of quietness and composure in the scene, the sense of a complete world—streams, mountains, plains, wide spaces of sky and sea—effortlessly displayed.

The Splendour of Greece

May 16

Holy Michael, the Archangel, defend us in the day of battle; be our safeguard against the wickedness and snares of the devil. May God rebuke him, we humbly pray; and do thou, Prince of the heavenly host, by the power of God, thrust down to hell Satan and all wicked spirits, who wander through the world for the ruin of souls.

Amen

When we are frightened by mortal or immortal foes, I like to think of Saint Michael defending me as I know he does.

May 17

A father complained to the Baalshem that his son had forsaken God. "What, Rabbi, shall I do?"

"Love him more than ever," was the Baalshem's reply.

Hasidic Story

May 18

I am so happy that we had those days,
Wind in our faces, and a cloudless sky.
I am so happy that we had those nights,
Do you remember how the moonlight made you sigh?
Every note I hear, each shaft of sun,
Reminds me of something we have done.
Music which echoes down the years,
Music of laughter with a touch of tears.
Your hand in mine, the times we talked together,
Those hours are mine, for ever and for ever.

I wrote this when someone I loved very deeply died. How hard it is in the first agony of loss to remember that while they have gone, all that they were remains. No one can take away from us, or spoil, those enchanted hours and days.

May 19

Wilt thou forgive that sin, with which I have won
Others to sin, and made my sin their door?

JOHN DONNE

*This is a prayer we should all pray. How easy to say: "What I do is
my own business and no one else's." But it is not true! We all
influence others, we all set an example, large or small. God save us
from helping others to sin!*

May 20

In 1939 the young men of Great Britain, as in 1914, said
with one voice:

> Comfort, content, delight—
> The ages slow-bought gain—
> They shrivelled in a night,
> Only ourselves remain
> To face the naked days
> In silent fortitude,
> Through perils and dismays
> Renewed and re-renewed.
> No easy hopes or lies
> Shall bring us to our goal,
> But with sacrifice
> Of body, will and soul.
> There is but one task for all—
> Our life for each to give.
> Who stands if Freedom fall?
> Who dies if England live?

RUDYARD KIPLING

May 21

I heard the beating of Death's wings,
I sought with groping hands escape
From all I knew without, within,
    Of life.

I am that pulse of moving life;
I am the river and its source;
Life cannot end, nor death begin
    In me.

May 22

Since well I know that everything which
seems real is not so,
Must I also know—dreams are not
dreams?

This comes from Zen Buddhism, whose followers know that life is not a beginning and an end. It is a chain of many links and our memories often wake and see one very clearly.

May 23

How often have we heard from our daily press that happiness is not news! Nevertheless, happiness persists. A broken marriage may hit the headlines, a good juicy murder is sure of them; but behind the casement curtains of suburban villas, in the little grey stone crofts and also in the big unwieldly country mansions are happy devoted couples who spend their lives in domestic contentment, who never see their names in print, and who would not have it otherwise.

May 24

Christ is the morning star who,
when the darkness of this world is past,
brings to his saints
the promise of the light of life
and opens everlasting day.

THE VENERABLE BEDE

May 25

He went to the windows of those who slept,
And over each pane, like a fairy, crept;
Wherever he breathed, wherever he stopped,
By the light of the morn were seen
Most beautiful things; there were flowers and trees;
There were bevies of birds, and swarms of bees;
There were cities, with temples and towers; and these
All pictured in silver sheen!

HANNAH FLAGG GOULD

*If we ever doubted that the Creator is an artist look into the garden
after a sharp frost. The luminous, glittering loveliness which has been
given to every tree, every weed and every blade of grass could not be
copied by the greatest jeweller in the world. Each tiny star of frost is
an exquisite prayer.*

May 26

That man, I trow, is doubly curst,
Who of the best doth make the worst;
And he I'm sure is doubly blest,
Who of the worst can make the best;
To sit and sorrow and complain,
Is adding folly to our pain.

WILLIAM COMBE

I always say to myself, "Don't complain," and I try never, never to be the conveyor of bad news. I try always to encourage, to give hope and comfort, but sometimes frankness is the spur to a better effort.

May 27

This world is not the only world. Every soul has existed from the beginning; it has therefore passed through some worlds already and will pass through others before it reaches the final consummation.

It comes into this world strengthened by the victories or weathered by the defects of its previous life.

Its place in the world as a vessel appointed to honour or dishonour is determined by its previous merits or demerits. Its work in this world determines its place in the world which is to follow this.

ORIGEN

May 28

Some say the age of chivalry is past, that the spirit of romance is dead. The age of chivalry is never past, so long as there is a wrong left.

CHARLES KINGSLEY

How many wrongs we see every day and quickly pass by on the other side. I pray for courage to use the weapons of my heart and soul to combat them.

May 29

For the reality of life, we learn too late, is in the living tissue of it from day to day, not in the expectation of better nor in the fear of worse. Those two things, to be always looking ahead, and to worry over things that haven't yet happened, and very likely won't happen—those take the very essence out of life.

STEPHEN LEACOCK

May 30

Live while you live, the epicure would say,
And seize the pleasures of the present day;
Live while you live, the sacred preacher cries,
And give to God each moment as it flies.
Lord, in my view let both united be;
I live in pleasure when I live to thee.

PHILIP DODDRIDGE

One need not be unhappy or starve to be good. I believe that we are put into this world to live fully, just as the man in the Bible was told to use all his talents. Nothing is more depressing than people who deliberately martyr themselves by refusing the joys of life.

May 31

I believe that, for those who have attained true enlightenment, supernormal powers are available, but that in all the universe there is no possibility of the breaking of natural law, but only of understanding and using its supernormal possibilities. I believe that grief is ignorance. I believe our sole prayer should be:

"From the unreal lead us to the Real.
From our blindness lead us to light.
From evolution lead us to perfection."

L. ADAMS BECK, *The House of Fulfilment*

June

June 1

Remember, O glorious and Good Saint Anne, that never was it known that anyone who fled to thy protection, implored thy help, and sought thy intercession, was left unaided.

Inspired by this confidence, behold, I cast myself at thy feet, and beseech thee, by thy great prerogative of being the Mother of the Queen of Heaven and the Grandmother of Jesus, come to my aid with thy powerful intercession, and obtain from Almighty God through the ever Blessed Virgin Mary, this special favour which I beg of thee . . . .

Cease not to intercede for me until, through Divine Mercy, my request may be granted. Above all, obtain for me the grace one day to behold my God face to face and with thee and Mary and all the Saints praise and bless Him through all eternity.

Amen

My mother, who was a Catholic, believed that Saint Anne listened to her prayers for anything that affected the family. This prayer is for mothers who worry over their children, and which mother does not long to protect them?

June 2

My heart's in the Highlands, my heart is not here,
My heart's in the Highlands, a-chasing the deer;
Chasing the wild deer, and following the roe—
My heart's in the Highlands, wherever I go.

ROBERT BURNS

*This well-known verse of Robert Burns tells us that our home, or
rather the place we love best, is always with us, wherever we may be,
in whatever circumstances we find ourselves.*

*We may not be aware of it, but it is our security and the foundation
on which we build character and personality. As a mother I pray
every day that my home may mean all that is fine, good, and inspiring
to my children.*

June 3

I will reveal to you a love potion, without medicine,
without herbs, without any witch's magic; if you want to be
loved, then *love*.

Hecaton of Rhodes

June 4

*Raise your hat, open the door
Yes, she really loves you more!
Bring her flowers, praise her dress,
Rob the bank—she couldn't care less!*

Kiss her good-morning, kiss her good-night,
On her eyes there's a child's delight
Whisper your love, through care and strife
She'll be faithful all through your life.

To be appreciated is the foundation-stone of a happy marriage. A woman wants to be told that she is loved not once but every minute, every day, every year of her life.

June 5

There is a road, steep and thorny, beset with perils of every kind—but yet a road; and it leads to the Heart of the Universe. I can tell you how to find Those who will show you the secret gateway that leads inward only, and closes fast behind the neophyte for evermore.

There is no danger that dauntless courage cannot conquer. There is no trial that spotless purity cannot pass through. There is no difficulty that strong intellect cannot surmount.

For those who win onwards, there is reward past all telling: the power to bless and save humanity. For those who fail, there are other lives in which success may come.

H. P. BLAVATSKY

June 6

We are told, "Let not the sun go down on your wrath." This, of course, is best; but, as it generally does, I would add, Never act or write till it has done so. This rule has saved me from many an act of folly. It is wonderful what a different view we take of the same event four-and-twenty hours after it has happened.

SYDNEY SMITH

I brought up my family on this motto, and we always apologize before we go to sleep. That is why as a family we are very close and very happy.

June 7

There came a time, perhaps in the ninth century B.C., when rumours of a young and handsome god armed with a bow of gold reached the mainland of Greece. He was a god who combined exquisite grace with a sense of quiet ruthlessness. He had been a sun-god and wore the spiked crown of the sun, but in some mysterious barely discernible way he had stepped down from his chariot to move among men, while remaining in the heavens.

He announced the new law that the earth belonged to the creators of music and poetry. He was no muscle-bound Hercules straining after victories of the flesh; his victories were those of the sunlit mind and the contemplative spirit.

The Splendour of Greece

June 8

I know that love makes all things equal: I have heard
By mine own heart this joyous truth averred,—
The spirit of the worm beneath the sod,
In love and worship, blends itself with God.

SHELLEY

June 9

O Father in Heaven, Who through Saint Therese of the Child Jesus, dost desire to remind the world of the merciful Love that fills Thy Heart, and the childlike trust we should have in Thee, humbly we thank Thee for having crowned with so great glory Thine ever faithful child, and for giving her wondrous power to bring unto Thee, day by day, innumerable souls who will praise Thee eternally.

Holy "Little Flower" remember thy promise to do good upon earth, shower down thy roses on those who invoke thee, and obtain for us from God the graces we hope for from His infinite goodness.

Amen

I have travelled all over the world and I always carry with me a medallion of Saint Therese and a tiny piece of cloth which had touched the body of the Saint, given me by the nuns at the Convent of Lisieux. No one can help but be moved by the promise of this young Nun who said: "I will spend my Heaven in doing Good upon Earth."

June 10

Myconos is a promise of Paradise. There comes a time when those spotless white bulidings have the power to haunt the soul.

Walking along those streets at noon, in the silence, you have the feeling that the world has suddenly come to an end, caught under a spell. Sometimes an old woman can be seen with bucket and brush, whitewashing the marble street, or a rubber-tyred push-cart comes silently by, with water from the sweet wells in the hills. Over the whiteness and the silence the pink domes of the churches rise like a benediction.

The Splendour of Greece

June 11

> Be thou a bright flame before me,
> Be thou a guiding star above me,
> Be thou a smooth path below me,
> Be thou a kindly shepherd behind me,
> Today—tonight—and forever.

SAINT COLUMBA OF IONA

June 12

I believe, absolutely, in the divine purpose of life. I think that every man and every woman has something to add to the stream of a nation's life; and every nation has its particular part to play with the other nations of the world in the general advance of mankind. As persons, as nations, we have different talents, different characters.

The Years of Opportunity

June 13

> *The world was unknown, a mysterious place,*
> *An adventure to move, to breathe in the sun.*
> *To get to the top was only a race*
> *Anyone could run.*
>
> *That was youth, when everything was new,*
> *Full of ideals and faith a vivid flame,*
> *Unspoilt, untired and courageous too,*
> *Living a game.*
>
> *Slowly the idols fall, bitter to know,*
> *That friends no longer friendly, envy, defame.*
> *Tired of the battle, getting old and slow*
> *Until we rise again.*

How little we appreciate our youth, how profligate we are with the years as they fly by. Only as we grow older do we cherish every hour, every minute of each day because the sands are running out.

June 14

If the little cowboy who acted as a guide to Bülow, Blücher's lieutenant, had advised to debouch from the forest above Frischermont rather than below Plancenoit, the shaping of the nineteenth century would perhaps have been different. Napoleon would have won the Battle of Waterloo. By any other road then below Plancenoit, the Prussian army would have brought up at a ravine impassable for artillery, and Bülow would not have arrived.

VICTOR HUGO

This story shows us how very important the smallest action by the smallest person can be. I often look back at my life and see how one casual thing I did had long-reaching consequences on many other people's lives.

June 15

What is the joy of Heaven but improvement in the things of the Spirit?

WILLIAM BLAKE

June 16

There's frost in the air and the leafless trees
Lift skeleton fingers toward the sky.
Your cruelty has brought me to my knees,
I am too cold and numb to cry.

Where have I failed you? What have I done,
That you should take your love from me?
Bleak and dark without the sun,
I'm frozen now 'till eternity.

*Love is the sun of a woman's life, without it she withers, grows old,
and something tender and beautiful within her dies.*

June 17

A lonely walk,
A quiet talk,
A grain of sand,
A soft white hand,
A child's new toy,
A moment's joy,
A new day's dawn,
A tottering fawn,
A cloud above,
Spring's new love,
A breath of air,
A silent prayer,
A gentle nod,
This is God.

ROBERT M. WARNER

June 18

I love the silver of the mist of dawn,
I love the shadows underneath the trees,
I love the softness of the velvet lawn,
The fragrance of syringa on the breeze.

I am so lonely without you here,
You who loved everything the garden grew.
The birds, the flowers are very dear,
But it's an empty beauty without you.

If we love someone, there is always a special place with which they are connected and where their personality remains. For some the snow-topped mountains, the turbulent sea against white cliffs or the music of a special tune. For my husband it was the garden.

June 19

Lead me from the unreal to the Real.
Lead me from darkness to Light.
Lead me from the mortal to the Immortal.

June 20

But prayer, after all, whether it is worship or contemplation or supplication, is only thought. It is man's thoughts which make him what he is. There lies the danger of life in cities in modern rush existence. Physical things leave little time for the spiritual, and yet to pray for physical benefits is better than not to pray at all.

RONALD CARTLAND

June 21

To sin against a fellow-man is worse than to sin against the Creator. The man you harmed may have gone to an unknown place, and you may lose the opportunity to beg his forgiveness. The Lord, however, is everywhere and you can always find Him when you seek Him.

A Hasidic Rabbi

June 22

The rustle of leaves in the banyan tree
As it shelters the old men from the sun.
Wood smoke and the smell of ghee,
White bullocks homeward come.
Beauty and misery side by side,
Famine and cholera, fear and strife.
Yet underneath the mystic tide
Of hope and faith which lifts each life
Towards Nirvana.

There is something in the non-attachment and fatalism of Buddhism which incites the desire for enlightenment which lies within all of us. What is the unknown? What part do we play in the secrets of the Universe? Is reincarnation the answer? In the serene face of Buddha we see the fulfilment of the soul.

June 23

In 1940–1945 there was among the young men a joie de vivre *or what was almost a delight in the adventures of war. Boys of twenty who would have been clerks in an office or apprentices "Sir-ing" their elders and betters were high ranking and highly decorated overnight. If nothing more, they were as they sped through the skies gods supremely conscious of their omnipotence and their power to take life or give their own.*

For twenty years you lived and laughed and played
Your glowing youth, and all who knew you laid
Returning tribute at your winged feet
That danced so blithely down the golden street
Where all are good companions; in the sun
You lived and laughed and played, and found it fun.

I was not with you on your last long flight
Through what tempestuous skies, through what black night,
But I would wager all that you were gay
And smiling as they pulled the chocks away—
You made your life a party to the end
And even Death must call you now his friend.

June 24

The real wealth of England was the character of her people. To impair it was national suicide. Neither profits nor utopian theories could ever justify a policy so short-sighted.

"A domestic oligarchy under the guise of Liberalism, is denationalizing England," Disraeli wrote in 1840, at the outset of his political career: "Hitherto we have been preserved from the effects of the folly of modern legislation by the wisdom of our ancient manners. The national character may yet save the Empire. The national character is more important than the Great Charter or trial by jury."

On the dusty roads from Mons to Marne river, in the blood-stained agony of Somme and Passchendaele, on Dunkirk Beach and in the skies above the Channel, the truth of that century-old prediction became clear.

ARTHUR BRYANT

June 25

Courage is rightly esteemed the first of human qualities because it is the quality which guarantees all others.

WINSTON CHURCHILL

Moral courage is often far more difficult than physical courage. To attack what one's heart tells one is wrong, knowing it will be extremely unpopular, requires the help of God.

June 26

Pindar tells the story of how the gods waited until Apollo was driving his sun-chariot across the heavens before they drew lots to divide up the earth among themselves. When Apollo learned what had happened, he stormed into the assembly of the gods and demanded that the earth should be divided up again, but at that moment he espied an island lurking at the bottom of the sea.

He was so astonished by the beauty of the island that he offered to let all the other gods keep their possessions as long as this island was given to him. "Then the island was lifted into the bright air and given to the father of the scorching rays and the driver of the fire-breathing horses."

The Splendour of Greece

June 27

When I build castles in the air,
Void of sorrow, void of fear.

ROBERT BURTON

We all do this. Our day-dreams, our imaginative flights are filled with happiness, motivated with love so eventually there is the happy ending! And these I promise do come true.

June 28

Would you sail away from the gloomy world
To the Land of Dreams Come True?
Then see the crimson sails unfurl,
The riding ropes undo.

Away to the Valley of Might Have Been
And the Fields of Laughing Hours,
Over the Hills of Wonders Seen,
And the bogs of Passion Flowers.
To linger awhile in Memory's Cave
Watching a gentle tide
Wash the wounds of fortune's slave
And those who have "always tried."
Blood-red sails on an emerald sea
And a silver moon above
The good ship Ended Happily,
Bound for the Land of Love.

Poems express the mystic, sensitive, secret things which we find it hard to put into prose. I often think that only the young and unspoilt heart really understands this fairy quality of poetry.

June 29

There is no merit in being young. There is immense opportunity.

RONALD CARTLAND

June 30

Lord, on you I call for help against my blind and senseless torment, since you alone can renew inwardly and outwardly my mind, my will, and my strength, which are weak.

MICHELANGELO

When we remember how strong, how brilliant, how versatile Michelangelo was, and how great were his achievements, this humble prayer is not only revealing but very, very inspiring.

July

July 1

Most amiable Lord Jesus, who didst become a little Child for us, and wouldst be born for us in a stable to deliver us from the darkness of sin, to draw us to Thee, and to enkindle us with Thy holy love, we adore Thee as our Creator and Redeemer, we acknowledge Thee and want Thee to be our King and sovereign Lord, and we offer Thee, as a tribute, all the affections of our God, vouchsafe to accept this offering, and that it may be less unworthy of Thee, pardon our sins, enlighten and inflame us with that holy fire, which Thou didst bring upon earth to kindle in our hearts. May thus our souls become a perpetual sacrifice to Thy honour, and ever seek Thy greater glory here below that we may, one day, enjoy Thy infinite beauty in Heaven.

Amen

I received this prayer when I saw the celebrated Statue of the Divine Infant which was carved in Jerusalem from the wood of the olive trees of Gethsemane in the fifteenth century by a member of the Franciscan Order. Brought to the Capitoline Hill, Rome, it is now visited by Catholics all over the world, owing to the innumerable favours the Divine Infant has bestowed on those who pray to Him. The Statue was crowned by the Vatican Chapter on May 2, 1897.

July 2

Health is a gift which comes from God,
But don't you think it's extremely odd?
How we take it for granted, until the day
When it's lost! And then we begin to pray
To God.

We expect good health to be free like the air and sunshine. But how grateful we should be for it to God, who gave man the most amazing machine in the world—a body.

July 3

I have lived and I have loved;
I have waked and I have slept;
I have sung and I have danced;
I have smiled and I have wept;
I have won and wasted treasure;
I have had my fill of pleasure;
And all these things were weariness,
And some of them were dreariness.
And all these things, but two things,
Were emptiness and pain;
And Love—it was the best of them;
And Sleep—worth all the rest of them.

Have you ever thought how grateful we should be for sleep, and how important it is in our lives? We take it for granted unless it eludes us and then we make a terrible fuss.

Never induce sleep artificially; droughts and tablets rot the brain. But take honey—God's most mystic food, and say a prayer—you will sleep.

July 4

> For a thousand years, 'neath a thousand skies,
>   Night has brought me love;
> Therefore the old, old longing rise
>   As the light grows dim above.
>
> Therefore, now that the shadows close,
>   And the mists rise weird and white,
> While the air is scented with musk and rose;
>   Magic with silver light.
>
> I long for love; will you grant me some?
>   Day is over at last.
> Come, as lovers have always come,
> Softly, as lovers have always come,
>   Through the long forgotten Past.
>
> *The Garden of Karma*

July 5

I know nothing more inspiring than the atmosphere of some of the Catholic Churches in France and Austria. One feels drawn to pray. Often they are dark and there is only the flicker of lighted candles to reveal the sweet face of Our Lady, of an ancient statue mellowed with time and the reflection on old brass and silver worn smooth by the care of the faithful.

One feels very near there to the Compassionate Heart of God, very close to the communion of Saints. Ronald and I always said that to get to know a foreign country one must pray in its Churches and eat in its cafés.

July 6

Write it on your heart that every day is the best day in the year. No man has learned anything rightly until he knows that every day is Doomsday.

RALPH WALDO EMERSON

"Live every minute to its full" has always been my motto, but then I was born in July and those people always want everything done immediately—if possible, yesterday.

July 7

A perfect world, without any need of our assistance, where everything is to be had for the asking, who wants it? Who, even if it were possible, could bear with it? Without successes or failure, without tears or laughter, without passions or interests? Action and endeavour are in the marrow of our bones.

W. MACNEILE DIXON

July 8

Nothing is voiceless in the world; God hears always
In all created things His echo and His praise.

ANGELUS SILESIUS

July 9

Flowers—fragrant and perfect—crimson, pink, and white,
Carnations, roses of every glowing hue.
Yellow-centred lilies—angels to light,
The chapels dedicated to La Mère de Dieu.

Flowers are a hand which comes to us from God,
When all is dark and we're beset with fear,
When evil steeps around us like a fog,
A flower will tell us help is always near.

How hard to choose, and to wonder how
Money can buy the glory of the sun!
In the dark, barren days of winter now
The fragrant color and my heart are one.

Nice Flower Market is a poem of beauty. Napoleon Bonaparte used to
have flowers sent from Nice to Paris every week and no one who has
wandered from stall to stall intoxicated by the scent and beauty can be
surprised at his extravagance.

July 10

There is but one salvation for a tired soul; love for another
person—for what is love, but—the lover makes the soul of his
beloved his sphere and they are one in spirit.

JOSÉ ORTEGA Y GASSET

July 11

There at last we lay
On beds of scented rushes and fresh vine-leaves,
While elms and poplars murmured overhead.
From the Cave of the Nymphs came the whisper
    of a spring,
And from the shady boughs came the chatter
    of dusky cicadas.
The voice of the turtle echoed from the thick
    thorn-brakes.
Doves were moaning, larks and finches were
    singing,
While over the running water hovered the bees.
Pears fell at our feet, apples rolled at
    our sides,
All things were fragrant with harvest and
    ripeness.

THEOCRITUS

July 12

*And there are those
Through whom the stream flows slowly,
Often dim and grey, but never still.
Its flow unceasing, ceaseless,
Till—as dawn breaks in a sable sky—
The purpose of its moving stands revealed,
The path of God—the leaping flame of life.*

I was suddenly vividly aware how each of us transmit the life-force through ourselves out towards the world. The same divine, radiant, glorious, eternal fire burns within us all, and yet how cruelly we can distort its power through our own ignorance or evil.

July 13

Be good, sweet maid, and let who will be clever:
Do lovely things, not dream them, all day long;
And so make Life, and Death, and that For Ever,
　　One grand sweet song.

CHARLES KINGSLEY

This has been quoted perhaps more than any poem since Canon Kingsley wrote it in the last century. That does not make it any less a message we should remember and follow. "Do lovely things—not dream them." That should be ambition, "to do" when there is so much to be done.

July 14

But (when so sad thou canst not sadder)
Cry; and upon thy so sore loss
Shall shine the traffic of Jacob's ladder
Pitched betwixt Heaven and Charing Cross.

Yea, in the night, my Soul, my daughter,
Cry,—clinging Heaven by the hems;
And lo, Christ walking on the water
Not of Gennesareth, but Thames.

FRANCIS THOMPSON

July 15

Little drops of water, little grains of sand,
Make the mighty ocean, and the pleasant land,
So the little minutes, humble though they be,
Make the mighty ages of eternity.

JULIA CARNEY

Nothing is too little to be important. Like the sparrow which fell to the ground, and the grain of mustard seed.

July 16

Mountains, oceans, plants, and the rest can communicate with us sometimes more intimately and nearly than any human voice. That was what Wordsworth meant by his spirit in the woods, what the Greeks meant by their Oreads, the mountain-haunting nymphs; their tree-dwellers; and beyond them the universal Pan, the collective being of them all.

Beliefs which I had half loved, half gently derided as myths, turned another face on me now, revealing their exquisite truth beyond all groping words. They are myths only because they attempt to reveal in impossible words what can only be known by disciplined intuition.

The House of Fulfilment

July 17

> For fable is Love's world, his home, his
> birthplace;
> Delightedly dwells he 'mong fays and
> talismans,
> And spirits; and delightedly believes
> Divinities, being himself divine.
>
> SAMUEL TAYLOR COLERIDGE

When I am in love, all the fairy tales come true for he is Prince Charming, and a magic wand has made me beautiful enough for him. That is Love's divine power to lift us upward toward Paradise.

July 18

As cloth when analysed is found to be nothing but thread, even so this universe, properly considered, is nothing but the One.

July 19

I swear by Apollo the Healer, by Asclepius, by Health and all the powers of healing, and I call to witness all the gods and goddesses that I may keep this Oath and Promise to the best of my ability and judgement.

To my master in the healing art I shall pay the same respect as to my parents, and I shall share my life with him and pay all my debts to him. I shall regard his sons as my brothers, and I shall teach them the healing art if they desire to learn it, without fee or contract. I shall hand on precepts, lectures and all other learning to my sons, to my master's sons and to those pupils who are duly apprenticed and sworn, and to no others. I will use my power to help the sick to the best of my ability and judgement. I will abstain from harming or wronging any man.

I will not give a fatal draught to anyone, even if it is demanded of me, nor will I suggest the giving of the draught. I will give no woman the means of procuring an abortion.

I will be chaste and holy in my life and actions.

I will not cut, even for the stone, but I will leave all cutting to the practitioners of the craft.

Whenever I enter a house, I shall help the sick, and never shall I do any harm or injury. I will not indulge in sexual union with the bodies of women or men, whether free or slaves.

Whatever I see or hear, either in my profession or in private, I shall never divulge. All secrets shall be safe with me.

If therefore I observe this Oath, may prosperity come to me and may I earn good repute among men through all the ages. If I break the Oath, may I receive the punishment given to all transgressors.

The Oath of Hippocrates

July 20

Life may be short, but a smile takes but a second.

Arab Saying

July 21

> HE *How beautiful you were,*
> *How soft your skin, your hair,*
> *Your youth's sweet grace!*
> *Yet now the love-lines on your face*
> *Make you more fair.*
>
> SHE *How handsome you were,*
> *How passionate, how strong;*
> *Making love the whole night long.*
> *Yet now your hair is sparse and grey,*
> *I love you more in every way.*

It was Bernard Shaw who said: "Love was too good for the young."
As we grow older we appreciate love more and are grateful for it. The
middle-aged know more about love than careless youth.

July 22

Swiftly walk o'er the western wave,
    Spirit of Night!
Out of the misty eastern cave,
Where, all the long and lone daylight,
Thou movest dreams of joy and fear,
Which make thee terrible and dear.—
    Swift be thy flight!

Wrap thy form in a mantle grey,
    Star-inwrought!
Blind with thine hair the eyes of Day;
Kiss her until she be wearied out,
Then wander o'er city, and sea, and land,
Touching all with thine opiate wand—
    Come, long-sought!

SHELLEY

July 23

Some said, John, print it; others said,
    Not so;
Some said, It might do good; others said,
    No.

JOHN BUNYAN

The world might have lost The Pilgrim's Progress *because in all our lives there are the "No" people. "Better not!" . . . "leave well alone" . . . "say nothing; it is safer!" Never listen to them; they are the faceless beige people who are of no more importance than the dust.*

117

July 24

I hold it true that thoughts are things
Endowed with bodies, breath and wings,
And that we send them forth to fill
The world with good results—or ill.

Then let your secret thoughts be fair;
They have a vital part and share
In shaping worlds and moulding fate—
God's system is so intricate.

ELLA WHEELER WILCOX

July 25

I could write down twenty cases, wherein I wished God had done otherwise than He did; but which I now see, had I my own will, would have led to extensive mischief; the life of a Christian is a life of paradoxes.

LORD BURLEIGH

I think we can all say the same when we look back into the past. God does know best so often and so positively that it makes me think carefully before I pray desperately for something I want. After all, He can see into the future, which I am unable to do.

July 26

Yet nature's charms—the hills and woods—
The sweeping vales and foaming floods—
Are free alike to all.

ROBERT BURNS

I think that all great reformers, all creative writers, all men and women with intelligence need the quietness and glory of Nature in which to recharge themselves. Just as some American Indians embrace a tree thinking they draw the life-force from it, so we need to draw sustenance from the air, the earth, the woods, the flowers. Christ went into the wilderness, Buddha to the forest, for strength.

July 27

The Greeks saw in the morning star a terrible divinity, who was very beautiful. They saw holiness wherever they walked. They saw it in little things. It was in the girl singing in the cornfield and in the young woman going down to the well and in the child riding for the first time on his father's shoulders; and there was the same holiness in the shape of the Parthenon, for that too was beautiful.

Holiness must come again; it has been too long from the earth. That is why for many generations to come men will return to the springs—to the splendour of Greece and the shattering light rising over the snow-white island of Apollo.

The Splendour of Greece

July 28

The utter joy of that First Love
No later love has given,
When while the skies grew light above,
We entered into Heaven.

The Garden of Karma

July 29

Saint Jude, glorious Apostle, faithful servant and friend of Jesus! the name of the traitor has caused thee to be forgotten by many, but the Church honours and invokes thee universally as the patron of hopeless cases—of matters despaired of. Pray for me who am so miserable; make use, I implore thee, of that particular privilege accorded to thee, to bring visible and speedy help where help is almost despaired of. Come to my assistance in this great need that I may receive the consolation and succour of heaven in all my necessities, tribulations, and sufferings, particularly . . . (here make your request), and that I may bless God with thee and all the elect throughout eternity.

I promise thee, O blessed Jude, to be ever mindful of this great favor, and I will never cease to honor thee as my special and powerful patron and do all in my power to encourage devotion to thee.

Amen

This prayer has never failed to help in desperate cases when I have almost despaired of finding a solution. I have found that an intercession to Saint Jude is, in fact, the most powerful prayer one can make.

July 30

> The gold of the sun and the silver stream,
> The purple heather a'top the moor,
> The wind to carry a beggar's dream
> Up the rainbow to Heaven's door.
> The earth's your bed and the sky's your roof,
> Someone you love to walk beside.
> They who matter, they know the truth,
> Every beggar who wishes can ride.

It is thought which counts in life, for what you think, you want; what you want, you get. I believe that our subconscious can bring us everything we desire—the question is, do we desire it enough?

July 31

> He:
> I seek a wife who will comfort me.
> I seek a girl who will laugh with me.
> I seek a woman warm to my touch,
> All in one—Do I ask too much?
>
> She:
> I seek a lover strong and free,
> I seek a man who will cosset me.
> I seek a husband to make a home
> All in one—for me alone.

It was Francis Bacon who wrote: "Wives are young men's mistresses, companions for middle age, and old men's nurses."

But every man wants a wife, mistress, and mother all in one woman. The amazing thing is that in millions of cases he gets it. But women also have their dreams!

August

August 1

A little more kindness, a little less creed;
A little more giving, a little less greed;
A little more smile, a little less frown;
A little less kicking a man when he's down;
A little more "we," and a little less "I,"
A little more laugh, a little less cry;
A little more flowers on the pathway of life
And fewer on graves at the end of the strife.

"Lines on American Authorship"

I love these American lines so full of good sense. I have always thought we should give flowers to the living, and not bother when they are dead.

August 2

The interiors of Elizabethan houses are always romantic and exciting. There are the long galleries with polished floors; the grand staircase with heraldic leopards sitting on top of the newels; the panelled rooms; the exquisitely designed plaster ceilings; the magnificent furniture of velvet, brocade, and needlework.

But it is strange to remember, when we grumble incessantly about the cold, how chilly our ancestors must have been. The best bedroom, with its great curtained bed, was usually situated at the end of a long gallery, and the long galleries, despite their huge fireplace, must have been cold and draughty. How grateful we should be for central heating.

August 3

The Moving Finger writes; and, having writ,
Moves on: nor all thy Piety nor Wit
    Shall lure it back to cancel half a Line,
Nor all thy Tears wash out a Word of it.

                                    EDWARD FITZGERALD

*I often regret a word spoken hastily and wish I could unsay it. I often
regret the kind word I forgot to say, or the praise I should have given
but left it too late.*

August 4

God who registers the cup
Of mere cold water, for His sake
To a disciple rendered up,
Disdains not His own thirst to slake
At the poorest love was ever offered:
And because it was my heart I proffered,
With true love trembling at the brim,
He suffers me to follow Him
For ever.

                                    ROBERT BROWNING

August 5

Must I go on through tears and pain
    Climbing to darkest peaks I cannot see?
Is man a creature born to grope in vain,
    Driven, directed, led, but never free?

What is the freedom of the mind?
Is it the rapture of an enlightened soul?
Only through suffering do we find
That love will make broken pieces whole.

Everyone suffers at some time in their life. One cannot escape it. Pain strengthens and fortifies the weak, unhappiness can show us new vistas which we never dreamt existed.

August 6

I love Love—though he has wings,
  And like light can flee,
But above all other things,
  Spirit, I love thee—
Thou art love and life! Oh, come,
Make once more my heart thy home.

SHELLEY

August 7

I love the darkness of your eyes,
I love the way you hold your head,
I love it when you sound so wise,
The way you always look well bred.

I love your fingers and your hands,
I love your walk, your narrow hips.
I love your arms, like steel bands,
But most of all I love your lips.

Women expect to be complimented and admired, but so do men. Love makes us want to give the people we love presents, and the most precious of all are words of love.

August 8

But there's wisdom in women,
    of more than they have known,
And thoughts go blowing through them,
    are wiser than their own.

RUPERT BROOKE

Women have an instinct for what is right and what is good, which can never be taught from books. It is because they think with love, and that is so much more powerful than logic.

August 9

One virtue stands out above all others; the constant striving upwards, wrestling with oneself, the unquenchable desire for greater purity, wisdom, goodness and love.

GOETHE

This is a virtue we all have. It is only when we are ashamed of being "good" because it is square or old-fashioned that we deny Christ within us, as Peter denied Him.

August 10

Because man is a key to the universe, because the mind of man is somehow linked with the Mind behind creation, the way to understanding of the Universe must finally embrace the thorough understanding of the mystery behind men.

PAUL BRUNTON

August 11

> Let me grow lovely, growing old,
> So many fine things do.
> Laces and ivory and gold
> And silks need not be new;
> And there is healing in old trees;
> Old streets a glamour hold;
> Why may not I, as well as these,
> Grow lovely, growing old?

K. W. BAKER

I believe that the elderly have so much to give to those who are younger. But it is as an example they are needed, not as competitors.

August 12

Lord, I know not what to ask of thee. Thou only knowest what I need. Thou lovest me better than I know how to love myself. Father, give to thy child that which he himself knows not how to ask. Smite or heal, depress me or raise me up: I adore all thy purposes without knowing them. I am silent; I offer myself up in sacrifice; I yield myself to thee; I would have no other desire than to accomplish thy will. Teach me to pray. Pray Thyself in me.

FRANÇOIS DE FÉNELON

August 13

There is a garden in her face,
Where roses and white lilies grow.

THOMAS CAMPION

When I read this I ask myself what flowers do others see in my face. Women should be the flowers of life—beautiful, fragrant, soft, and tender. For what could be more wonderful than the purity of the lily, the sensual loveliness of a rose?

August 14

Thy will is free:
Strong is the Soul, and wise, and beautiful:
The seeds of godlike power are in us still;
Gods are we, Bards, Saints, Heroes, if we will!

MATTHEW ARNOLD

We all know that if we are determined enough we get what we want. But we must set our sights high, to be really successful the goal must really be just out of reach!

August 15

Then give to the world the best you have:
And the best will come back to you.

MADELINE BRIDGES

This is a variation of "Cast your bread upon the water, and it will come back iced cake." It is true, I have proved it personally over and over again.

129

August 16

On a hill where the singing streams descended to the lake through mossy rocks, with gardens of tree-peonies inhabited by silver peacocks, was placed the Golden Palace of the Empress.

The curved Roofs of royal yellow porcelain diffused a sunshine of their own and were mirrored in the lake beneath like a more sumptuous day. Pleasure-boats, moored to the marble balustrades that surrounded the majestic lake, floates like hovering butterflies among the lotus blossoms that reared their pure chalices in the clear air. Pavilions of choicest lacquer, illustrating in golden pictures the histories of sages, awaited fair occupants rejoicing in the lute and wine-cup, but, save for the voices of birds and gentle tinkling of the crystal wind-bells, deep silence and emptiness reigned supreme.

L. ADAMS BECK

Beauty should be seen and shared. This description is of the Empress's Palace in the Forbidden Precincts of China, but we all have secret places in our own lives which we should share with those we love and those we might love.

August 17

You who speak of her beauty—have you seen her heart? You who see the cherry tree and do not know her soul—You have not seen her.

Japanese Poem

August 18

Be thou the rainbow to the storms of life!
The evening beam that smiles the clouds away,
And tints tomorrow with prophetic ray.

LORD BYRON

This is what every woman should be. Not only a sympathetic listener, but a rainbow of hope. That is what we all need when we are distressed, despondent, and afraid. Hope not only gives us the belief that we can try again, but convinces us that we will succeed.

August 19

Music of whispering trees
Hushed by the broad-winged breeze
Where shaken water gleams;
And evening radiance falling
With ready bird-notes calling.
O bear me safe through dark, you low-voiced streams.

I have no need to pray
That fear may pass away;
I scorn the growl and rumble of the fight
That summons me from cool
Silence of marsh and pool,
And yellow lilies islanded in light.
O river of stars and shadows, lead me through the night!

SIEGFRIED SASSOON

August 20

Lord Jesus Christ,
How often was I impatient, about to lose heart,
about to give up everything, about to
    seek the fearfully easy way out, despair,
But you never lost patience.
You bore a whole life of suffering to redeem
    even me.

KIERKEGAARD

August 21

We all have hidden in our hearts a secret shrine in which we have placed a picture of our ideal love. Like pilgrims, we search for the ecstasy, the rapture, and the wonder of real love that is both human and divine. This is what I have sought all my life.

August 22

Music strikes in me a deep fit of devotion, and a profound contemplation of the First Composer. There is something in it of Divinity more than the ear discovers.

SIR THOMAS BROWNE

Music is the easiest of the great Arts which will raise our minds towards God. This is because we all have music within us, and even as we breathe rhythmically, so our whole being is really responding to the melody of the Universe. I write to music, and when I listen I can hear the word I need to complete a sentence.

August 23

A garden is a lovesome thing, God wot!
Rose plot,
Fringed pool
Ferned grot—
The veriest school
of peace; and yet the fool
Contends that God is not.
Not God! in gardens! When the eye is cool!
Nay, but I have a sign;
'Tis very sure God walks in mine.

T. E. BROWN

In a garden, because it is filled with beauty, with the songs of birds and the fragrance of the flowers, it is easy to feel close to God and to talk to Him.

August 24

We know not Life's reason,
The length of its season,
    Know not if they know, the Great Ones above.
We none of us sought it,
And few could support it,
    Were it not gilt with the glamour of Love.

The Garden of Karma

August 25

Poems are made by fools like me,
But only God can make a tree.

JOYCE KILMER

When I first heard this beautiful song, whose author was killed in the war [World War I], I was moved to tears. It was so simple and yet so moving, and like Joyce Kilmer, "I think that I shall never see, a poem lovely as a tree."

August 26

Blessed is he who has found his work; let him ask no other blessedness.

THOMAS CARLYLE

It takes most people a long time and sometimes a lifetime to discover that they are happier when they are working. Most men have the idea that when they have nothing to do they will find contentment. This has been proved to be wrong by every man who retires, whatever his business.

Anyone who has brains is happy when he is using them, anyone who is creative is only complete when he is exercising that Divine gift.

August 27

We shall never plumb the depths and the ultimate mysteries of life. The only thing that really matters is what we make of our lives.

THORNTON WILDER

August 28

All the great men I have known in my life have been supremely sure of themselves, confident of what they wanted of life and believed fervently in their cause.

These qualities are essential for leadership, but I have also found that all really great men, like Winston Churchill, prayed and sought the help and guidance of God.

August 29

It is easy to have ideals and excuse oneself from allowing them to have any influence on one's life by complaining that they are too high, too splendid, for this world. Ideals must be related, closely related to the world in which we live. We live in this world. We strive to better ourselves. We strive to better the conditions of the world around us, as a development of ourselves. No Government can change a man's soul; the souls of men change Governments.

RONALD CARTLAND

August 30

I believe that all women, whether they know it or not, view life maternally. When they love a man they want to cosset and protect him from being hurt, mentally or physically, while the causes they sponsor are chosen because their warm, maternal hearts bleed when they see suffering and injustice.

August 31

And yet, as angels, in some brighter dreams,
  Call to the soul when man doth sleep,
So some strange thoughts transcend our wonted
themes,
  And into glory peep.

HENRY VAUGHAN

I often have dreams which bring me new ideas, but always when I want a new plot for a book, I pray and suddenly—sometimes at the last minute—it is there—everything as clear as if someone had told it to me, so all I have to do is the research and to get it down on paper.

September

September 1

I, John, who also am your brother, and companion in tribulation, and in the kingdom and patience of Jesus Christ, was in the isle that is called Patmos, for the word of God, and for the testimony of Jesus Christ. I was in the Spirit on the Lord's day, and heard behind me a great voice, as of a trumpet, saying, I am Alpha and Omega, the first and the last: and, What thou seest, write in a book, and send it unto the seven churches which are in Asia.

So, somewhere toward the end of the first century, in a cave in Patmos, wrote an old man who may have been the Beloved Disciple, in a mood of extraordinary excitement, which still makes our hearts beat faster.

September 2

In Chapter 21 of *Revelation*, John describes the City of God glittering with thousands of polished stones, gleaming like glass and shining like gold. Is this, as it seems to be, a vision based upon the island of Patmos in the dawn-light, when the storm is over and thousands of flooded springs and rivulets pour down the mountain-side, glistening on the red and purple porphyry?

At such moments the island might well seem to glow with an interior light. After describing the city with its gates of pearl and foundations of jasper, emerald, beryl, sardonyx, sapphire, and all the precious stones he can remember, John adds: "The city had no need of the sun, neither of the moon, to shine in it: for the glory of God did lighten it, and the Lamb is the light thereof."

The Splendour of Greece

September 3

He that piles up treasures has much to lose.

LAO-TSE

September 4

I remember, I remember,
The fir trees dark and high;
I used to think their slender tops
Were close against the sky;
It was a childish ignorance,
But now 'tis little joy
To know I'm further off from Heaven
Than when I was a boy.

THOMAS HOOD

The faith of a child is something which is never forgotten, and I know that what I learnt about God and the prayers I said when I was very young have helped and inspired me all through my life.

September 5

They shall grow not old, as we that are left grow old;
Age shall not weary them, nor the years condemn.
At the going down of the sun, and in the morning,
We will remember them.

LAURENCE BINYON

To those of us who have lost those we loved on the battlefield, or in an accident when their lifespan was not complete, these are wonderful words, bringing them vividly close to us.

September 6

For years you walked beside me every day,
For years you slept upon my bed.
You showed your love in every way,
I can't believe that you are dead.

If there's an after-life for me,
Then I'd be lonely without you.
I must be sure that you will be
With me, whatever I may do.

So I pray to God who made you and me,
Who in death swept us apart,
To book a place in the "Great To Be"
For a dog with a loving heart.

This was written to a Pekingese called Wong, who was with me for sixteen years. He was proud, independent, and obstinate, but loyal, loving, and whole-heartedly mine. Could anyone ask for more from a friend?

September 7

Dusting, darning, drudging, nothing is great or small,
Nothing is mean or irksome, love will hallow it all.
                                        WALTER CHALMERS SMITH

I have often said to housewives who have grumbled about the monotony of housework: "Your house is your Kingdom and all yours and you make it lovely for the man you love—think of it as a frame for yourself."

But it is love which makes a home, just as it is love which makes a marriage.

September 8

The spark of life within and without is ever the same.
In an atom is the whole Kingdom of God.
In one grain are numberless worlds.
There is but one principle in soul and body.
He who knows this must follow the mystery of nature.

Ancient Chinese Book

Life is the same whether it is in man or in a stone, and we know the scientists have found that stones live and breathe. That is how we know indisputably that there is no death, only our bodies crumble from age, but the life in it is part of the Eternal.

September 9

The bravest are surely those who have the clearest vision of what is before them, glory and danger alike, and yet notwithstanding go out to meet it.

PERICLES

September 10

A mind not to be changed by place or time
The mind is its own place, and in itself
Can make a heav'n of hell, a hell of Heav'n.
What matter where, if I be still the same.

JOHN MILTON

Of course we make our own Heaven and Hell, but in doing so we are not alone. There are not only the hosts of Heavenly beings on our side, but close to us all those we love and have loved, and who, wherever they may be, still love us.

141

September 11

As persons, as nations, we have different talents, different characters. Taken altogether, they make up the whole complete pattern of life—as many shades go to the making of a single colour.

RONALD CARTLAND

September 12

We are the Pilgrims, master; we shall go
   Always a little further; it may be
Beyond that last blue mountain barred with snow,
   Across that angry or that glimmering sea.

White on a throne or guarded in a cave,
   There lives a prophet who can understand
Why men were born: but surely we are brave,
   Who take the Golden Road to Samarkand.

HASSAN

Pilgrims in the past travelled many weary, difficult miles, but we know we can make the pilgrimage in our minds. It is often more difficult, it may be even more painful, but at the end of the journey there is the Samarkand we each one of us seek in our hearts.

September 13

They will come back, come back again,
  As long as the red earth rolls,
He never wasted a leaf or tree,
  Do you think he would squander souls?

RUDYARD KIPLING

I believe this is true. How could the personality, the character achieved in a long life die with a worn-out body? And how without this explanation could Mozart play the violin at the age of four and write a concerto when he was six?

September 14

The freshness, the eternal youth,
Of admiration sprung from truth;
From beauty infinitely growing
Upon a mind with love o'erflowing.

WILLIAM WORDSWORTH

Love does keep a woman beautiful and young whatever her age. All emotions leave their mark on the face of those who feel them. Hate makes us ugly, love makes us lovely.

September 15

How does Love speak?
In the proud spirit suddenly grown meek—
The haughty heart grown humble in the tender
And unnamed light that floods the world with splendour;

In the resemblance which the fond eyes trace
In all fair things to one beloved face;
In the shy touch of hands that thrill and tremble—
In looks and lips that can no more dissemble—
Thus doth Love speak.

ELLA WHEELER WILCOX

September 16

No coward soul is mine,
No trembler in the world's storm-troubled sphere;
I see Heaven's glories shine,
And Faith shines equal, arming me from Fear.

EMILY JANE BRONTË

Faith in God sustains and arms those who have it, and faith in what we know is right gives us courage to attempt the impossible and win.

September 17

He prayeth well, who loveth well
Both man and bird and beast.

He prayeth best, who loveth best
All things both great and small;
For the dear God, who loveth us,
He made and loveth all.

SAMUEL TAYLOR COLERIDEGE

There is so much sense in this bright little verse, for only a great overwhelming love could have created anything so fantastically wonderful as the Universe.

September 18

Man is made by his belief. As he believes, so he is.

Bhagavad-Gita

This is the ancient way of saying what you think today you become tomorrow.

September 19

Thy dawn, O Master of the World, thy dawn;
The hour the lilies open on the lawn,
The hour the grey wings pass beyond the mountains,
The hour of silence, when we hear the fountains,
The hour that dreams are brighter and winds colder,
The hour that young love wakes on a white shoulder,
O Master of the World, the Persian Dawn.

HASSAN

These words paint a picture that is so beautiful that it is to me very moving and therefore a prayer.

September 20

A pride there is of rank—a pride of birth,
A pride of learning, and a pride of purse,
A London pride—in short, there be on earth
A host of prides, some better and some worse;
But of all prides, since Lucifer's attaint,
The proudest swells a self-elected Saint.

THOMAS HOOD

We all detest the "holier-than-thou" person and how careful we must be not to become one of them.

September 21

Love knows no boundaries, no horizons, only fools try to restrict and express it. Love is life, fierce, impetuous, demanding. Love is soft, tender, and understanding. Love is man and woman complete in one person, in one Universe, created by one God.

September 22

> I have been here before,
> But when or how I cannot tell;
> I know the grass beyond the door,
> The sweet, keen smell,
> The sighing sound, the lights around the shore.

DANTE GABRIEL ROSSETTI

We have all known experiences like this. We have all been aware that we have seen and felt and known someone before.

September 23

As we see you centred in bright glory, beloved Saint Cecilia, we beg you to watch over us. The admirable examples of your heroic life, crowned by spotless lilies and crimson roses, enthral us. Obtain for us, through the intercession of Mary, our sweet heavenly Mother, the infinite mercy of God, that we may live according to the teachings of the Gospel, confound in this way the deceits of the world, so that we can tend with all our strength toward the eternal home awaiting us. Pray, that we may love without measure while on earth, so that we can love and be loved in the eternal, infinite beatitude of God.

Amen

I love the beauty of this prayer to Saint Cecilia and it is easy to picture her as lovely as the flowers with which she is crowned, giving us the same courage as she showed when she was martyred.

September 24

Of Courtesy—it is much less
Than courage of heart or holiness;
Yet in my walks it seems to me
That the Grace of God is in courtesy.

HILAIRE BELLOC

Courtesy or good manners are the flowers of life. I hate digging for "a heart of gold" under a rough exterior, and I will forgive men and women many wrongs if they do them with charm and elegance.

September 25

The kiss of the sun for pardon,
The song of the birds for mirth;
One is nearer God's Heart in a garden
Than anywhere else on earth.

DOROTHY FRANCES GURNEY

We've read this a thousand times, we've repeated it to ourselves, but it is true and it is not only what a garden gives us, but the love we give to it.

September 26

Millions of spiritual creatures walk the earth
Unseen, both when we wake and when we sleep.

JOHN MILTON

I have a ghost dog in my home. When I moved into my present home I had it blessed because I dislike ghosts. But a dog who I put to sleep because he had cancer of the throat is still with us—I have seen him many times and so have other people. I am sure he stays with us because he loves us.

September 27

Sleep is a death; O make me try
By sleeping, what it is to die;
And as gently lay my head
On my grave, as now my bed.

SIR THOMAS BROWNE

My mother, who died when she was ninety-eight, was a little afraid of dying. She thought it might be painful. She fell asleep watching and enjoying television.

September 28

You know him slightly. We, who knew him well,
Saw something in his soul you could not see.

ROBERT W. BUCHANAN

There is in everyone something deep, secret and wonderful, if we could but find it. Just as everyone has something beautiful about him. It may not be obvious, but no living person is really ugly. I sometimes seek for hidden beauty in strangers and find winged eyebrows, a dimple, or perfectly sculptured ears! I never draw a complete blank.

September 29

I must go down to the seas again, to the
lonely sea and the sky,
And all I ask is a tall ship and a star
to steer her by,

149

And the wheel's kick and the wind's song
  and the white sails shaking,
And a grey mist on the sea's face and
  grey dawn breaking.

JOHN MASEFIELD

This song has always moved me deeply. I cannot explain why because I do not like being on the sea—but whenever I hear it something within me rises like a wave and a prayer.

September 30

You can't keep trouble from coming, but
you needn't give it a chair to sit on.

Old Proverb

October

October 1

I still remember walking down the Notting Hill main road and observing the (extremely sordid) landscape with joy and astonishment. Even the movement of the traffic had something universal and sublime in it.

EVELYN UNDERHILL

The light of God comes to us unexpectedly, and suddenly the whole world is radiant and beautiful. This happened to me once in Greece, and I can still see vividly in my mind the glory of view which suddenly became Divine.

October 2

There are places on the earth where Holiness dwells, where benign influences rise from the earth and encompass those who walk on it. Those places are rare, and very often they are associated with crimes and sacrifice; so it is in Jerusalem, where crimes innumerable have been committed, though holiness remains. So it is too in Delos. Apollo was born there, and his influence still spreads across the world, like the ripples when a stone is flung into a pool. He did not die. He became the young Christ, the god came to earth, the radiance of his celestial journey still about him.

One imagines he came because he was needed, because he filled some desperate need for clarity, lucidity, and order.

The Splendour of Greece

October 3

Over Delos the air is a dancing, quivering flame, and all the islands around are like mirrors giving shape to the light, to the great blue dome of the Apollonian heaven.

Delos, then, is this light, this strange glitter and shining high up in the air, a mysterious quivering, the beating of silver wings, the whirling of silver wheels. There is this very rich, very pure light, never still, and when the eyes have grown accustomed to it, then at last the island loses its fragility, as a golden chalice seen through curtains and lit by flickering candles also loses its fragility after a while.

The Splendour of Greece

October 4

This is life: to keep
Steadfast to the light.
This is death: to leap
From the topmost height
Of ecstatic being straight into the night.

RUDOLF BESIER

October 5

When one is in love, one sees only the face of the man one loves, hears only his voice and the beat of his heart. Wherever we may be, even in a crowded room, we are alone because no one else has any importance. To me he is the only man and to him I am the only woman in the whole wide world.

October 6

> Though a man be soiled
> With the sins of a lifetime,
> Let him love me,
> Rightly resolved,
> In utter devotion:
> I see no sinner,
> That man is holy.
>
> *Bhagavad-Gita*

A woman who loves a man who loves her will always forgive the past. So wisely because it is the future which matters—a future with love.

October 7

Love makes the hovel to be a golden palace, scatters dancing and play over the wilderness, uncovers to us the light traces of the divinity; gives us a foretaste of heaven!

HOLTY

October 8

Even if you had failings, I should be forbearing. It is not love when one simply draws a beautiful picture in one's soul and endows it with every perfection; rather, this is love: to love people as we find them, and if they have weaknesses, to accept them with a heart filled with *love*.

CHARLOTTE TO SCHILLER

How often we try to change those we love instead of loving them more because they are as they are. That is real and true love.

October 9

Hands of invisible spirits touch the strings
Of that mysterious instrument, the soul.

HENRY W. LONGFELLOW

A soul is mysterious. Some people even say it does not exist, but I know when I am deeply moved by beauty, when music lifts me up towards the sky, it is my soul which responds. It is my soul, too, which makes me say "I believe," with a conviction beyond the confines of the heart. I believe my heart is mine, but my soul belongs to God.

October 10

Take time to read,
take time to think;
it is the road to wisdom.
Take time to laugh,
take time to love,
it is the road to being alive.
Take time to give,
take time to pray:
it is the way to God.

HENRY DRUMMOND

October 11

Delayed it may be for long years yet,
Through lives I shall traverse not a few.
Much is to learn and much to forget.

This ancient verse from India speaks of rebirth, and who can argue that we in this dimension have much to learn of today and much to lose of the past sins and mistakes of yesterday.

October 12

If I should die, think only this of me:
That there's some corner of a foreign field
That is for ever England.

RUPERT BROOKE

October 13

History is not merely a matter of facts and dates; it is far more exciting than that; it is a record of the accomplishment and frustration, the victory and the defeat, the torment, the sacrifice, and the achievement in a great many millions of individual lives.

It is you and I. We are a part of it. We make it. And what to me is so amazing is that history, like our own personal lives, appears to depend so carelessly on chance. We each of us have said over and over again: "If I hadn't gone to tea with the Vicar on that particular day . . . ." "If I hadn't missed my usual bus . . . my whole life would have been different."

When I look back I realize that if my Father—who didn't dance—hadn't gone to a ball, seen my Mother, and said, "That is the girl I am going to marry!" I mightn't have been born.

But is it really by chance? There is a pattern, and it is woven by a Power which guides us and which I believe knows how we can best develop and grow spiritually. Sometimes this is by suffering, but always by love.

October 14

Ay, call it holy ground,
    The soil where first they trod!
They have left unstained what there they found—
    Freedom to worship God!

                FELICIA DOROTHEA HEMANS

This was written on the landing of the Pilgrim Fathers in America. How extraordinary it seems that all these years later there is still religious intolerance in the world. But we too are intolerant in a thousand ways if people do not agree with what we believe to be right.

October 15

God comes down in the rain,
And the crop grows tall—
This is the country faith,
And the best of all.

October 16

My philosophy, as a Christian, rests on the belief that a man's life in this world is a preparation for the next; that the soul of man is more important than his body, and that as far as it is possible in the state of society in which he lives a man should be allowed to work out his destiny in his own way.

We have our ideals; but ideals, let us remember, if they are to have a real influence in our lives, must be related—closely related—to the world in which we dwell now. We live in the world as it is; we strive to better it; but we realize that the Kingdom of God is above and it is man's soul that will attain to it—not man's body.

RONALD CARTLAND

October 17

Do the work that's nearest,
 Though it's dull at whiles,
Helping, when we meet them,
Lame dogs over stiles.

CHARLES KINGSLEY

The Canon had the knack of putting the obvious into verse, and who would forget this truthful little rhyme?

So many people find their work dull—can we do anything to help them overcome the monotony of a soul-destroying treadmill? That, after all, is our "nearest work."

October 18

When something has happened, do not talk about it, it is hard to collect spilled water.

Chinese Wisdom

October 19

Let me arise and open the gate,
To breathe the wild warm air of the heath,
And to let in Love, and to let out Hate,
And anger at living, and scorn of Fate,
To let in Life, and to let out Death.

MARY MONTGOMERIE SINGLETON

There is a gate in all of us which we can open or keep closed. Often the bolts which prevent it from opening are the hatreds, the resentments, the spiteful thoughts which accumulate over the years.
   Open the gate, there is sunshine and love waiting to come in!

October 20

How seldom do we try to give love to the ordinary and commonplace activities of the day—the housework, the trudge to work, the pushing through crowds, the long wait for a bus. Yet if we force ourselves to do small things with love in our mind and heart, they can be transformed with the beauty which comes from within ourselves and illuminates them.

October 21

Go thou and seek the House of Prayer!
I to the woodlands wend, and there,
In lovely Nature see the God of Love.

ROBERT SOUTHEY

This poem, written on Sunday morning, reminds us that we do not have to go to Church to pray. Also that religion was created to help us, not us religion. All a Church can do is to help us to concentrate on God, which we often forget in the rush and bustle of the daily round.

But I find Him in the first glimmer of the sun, the mystery of the mist, the music of the wind, the patter of the rain, and in the beat of my heart.

October 22

Nothing in the world is single;
All things by a law divine
In one another's being mingle—
Why not I with thine?

SHELLEY

October 23

This is the miracle that happens every time to those who really love; the more they give, the more they possess of this precious nourishing love from which flowers and children have their strength and which could help all human beings if they would take it without doubting . . . .

RAINER MARIA RILKE

This is so true. I heard a famous singer say on television that she worked at her marriage every day of her life. To keep love not only alive but to help it grow, we must tend and feed it—cosset and of course love it.

October 24

I am convinced that as in art all is one inspiration, though separated in the world into painting, poetry, music and so forth, that the means of perception which we guess in dreams and know in the deeper states that lies below dreaming.

October 25

He opens an enchanted gate
For each untrodden ridge;
He cleaves the blue precipitate stair
Up the white domes of front and air,
And moulds the foam-snow bridge.
How small the earth to those wide eyes,
And the near welcome of the skies
How infinitely great.

GEOFFREY WINTHROP YOUNG

October 26

Do not wish to be anything but what you are, and try to be that perfectly.

FRANCIS OF SALES

I think when we try to be like someone else we deny God. The great miracle of creation is that out of the billion, trillion bodies in the world not one is exactly the same as another! Each of us is unique; how could we be anything but proud!

October 27

Be ye lamps unto yourselves,
Be your own reliance.
Hold to the truth within yourselves
As to the only lamp.

GAUTAMA BUDDHA

October 28

Ah Love! could thou and I with Fate conspire
To grasp this sorry Scheme of Things entire,
Would not we shatter it to bits—and then
Re-mould it nearer to the Heart's Desire.

EDWARD FITZGERALD

We have all wished at times to remold the world, to change it to suit
ourselves, to build a better one. But would it be any better?
If we eliminated, which I am sure we should, all the difficulties and
troubles, would our characters be any finer, would we be any better?
Perhaps we should lose our greatness, for the one thing which this
difficult, tempestuous world produces in us is courage, and courage is
the light which shines from the gods themselves.

October 29

The night has a thousand eyes,
And the day but one;
Yet the light of the bright world dies
With the setting sun.

The mind has a thousand eyes,
And the heart but one;
Yet the light of a whole life dies
When love is done.

F. W. BOURDILLON

Love is why we are born, how we should live, and when we die we find love in God.

October 30

Many friends will not profit, nor will strong helpers be able to assist, nor prudent counselors give a profitable answer, nor the books of the learned afford comfort, nor any precious substance deliver, nor any place, however retired and lovely, give shelter unless Thou, O Lord, Thyself dost stand by, help, strengthen, console, instruct, and guard us.

THOMAS À KEMPIS

October 31

'Tis heaven alone that is given away,
'Tis only God may be had for the asking.

J. R. LOWELL

If one had to pay it would be the most expensive and the most valuable thing on earth. But, rich or poor, high or low, we have only to speak to God in our own simple words and He is there listening to us.

November

November 1

But ah! In vain from Fate I fly,
For first, or last, as all must die,
So 'tis as much decreed above,
That first, or last, we all must love.

GEORGE GRANVILLE, LORD LANSDOWNE

No one has lived without loving someone. Our hearts are made to be given, even if hopelessly, to a man, woman, a child, or an animal. For only by loving do we grow spiritually.

November 2

There are mysteries about the Parthenon which no one has ever solved. Why is it that of all the buildings in the world this one alone, though ruined and damaged beyond repair, speaks with a clear, unhurried voice of its own perfection?

There are only a handful of authentically great buildings left in the world. In their different ways Santa Sophia in Constantinople, the Temple of Heaven in Peking, the Mosque of Sheikh Lutfullah in Ispahan, the Taj Mahal in Agra, and the Dome of the Rock in Jerusalem have achieved that perfection which is reserved only for the highest works of art, but none of them approaches the perfect dignity of the Parthenon, that utmost grandeur. There is something almost insolent in the way the Parthenon says quietly: "I have been worn to the bone, but I am the most living of all things."

The Splendour of Greece

November 3

Dear God, it is so hard for us not to be anxious,
we worry about work and money,
about food and health,
about weather and crops,
about war and politics,
about loving and being loved.
Show us how perfect love casts out fear.

MONICA FURLONG

November 4

Insomuch as Love grows in you so in you beauty grows.
For Love is the beauty of the Soul.

SAINT AUGUSTINE

*I have never known any woman who has not become beautiful with
love. It is like a brilliant light beneath the skin and radiates out to
everyone who sees her.*

November 5

Adoration to Krishna the Beloved, to the Flute-player
whose breath is the Divine, whose flute is the Heart of Man.
Adoration to him who, as the Lover of the Herd-maidens, is
the Soul among the Five Senses, who, as the Lover of Radha,
is the Divine that embraces the Soul.

L. ADAMS BECK

*Krishna is the Hindu God of Love, and his beauty and the music of his
flute, which is decorated with honey-bees, fills the legends of India with
an indescribable magic.*

167

November 6

> The pure soul
> Shall mount on native wings, disdaining little sport,
> And cut a path into the heaven of glory,
> Leaving a track of light for men to wonder at.
>
> WILLIAM BLAKE

Blake always saw the World behind the world, and here he describes it so vividly. We must look at what is around us not only with our eyes but with that perceptive instinct within us which belongs to the soul.

November 7

Each individual raises a standard for himself. Each man is a judge of his own progress, and in condemning the state of society in which he lives he convicts himself. But principles are static. The fundamentals of Christianity do not change. They are the rule by which one can measure the achievements or failures of the age.

RONALD CARTLAND

November 8

He prays well who is so absorbed with God that he does not know he is praying.

FRANCIS OF SALES

This is what I believe you will find in this book. The movement of your heart, the questions in your mind, the uplifting of your soul—it is all prayer.

November 9

Do I sleep? do I dream?
Do I wander and doubt?
Are things what they seem?
Or is visions about?

BRETT HART

*We all have moments of doubt, moments when we are alone and there
seems no answer to the questions which echo and re-echo in our heart.
But always the darkness fades, the veil lifts, and there with us all the
time is the World behind the world.*

November 10

I detect more good than evil in humanity.
Love lights more fires than hate extinguishes,
And men grow better as the world grows old.

ELLA WHEELER WILCOX

November 11

Nor second He, that rode sublime
   Upon the seraph-wings of Ecstasy,
   The secrets of th' abyss to spy.
He passed the flaming bounds of place and time:
The living throne, the sapphire-blaze
Where angels tremble, while they gaze.

THOMAS GRAY

*This was written of Milton, and his vision of Paradise Lost and
Paradise Regained can still show how we, like Adam, can lose our
divinity yet find it again.*

November 12

God goes out to those who come to meet him.

Russian Saying

November 13

When as a child I laughed and wept,
Time crept;
When, as a boy, I laughed and talked,
Time walked;
When I became a full-grown man,
Time ran;
As older still I daily grew,
Time flew;
Soon shall I find, in travelling on,
Time gone.
O Christ, wilt Thou have saved me then?
Amen.

HENRY TWELLS

This is so true, that it is strange so many of us waste precious time on foolish things. On quarrels with old friends, or taking umbrage over small things, or crying for the lost hours, months, and years that can never come again, or sulking and being bored.

All these things are Time wasted, while time spent in kindness, in sympathy and understanding, and most of all in loving, is Time gained.

November 14

> The hearts that on each other beat
>   From evening close to morning light,
> Have nights as good as they are sweet,
>   But never *say* good-night.

SHELLEY

November 15

My task which I am trying to achieve is, by the power of the written word, to make you hear, to make you feel—it is, before all, to make you *see*. That, and no more, and it is everything.

JOSEPH CONRAD

I do not enjoy a book which does not make me "see." It is the pictures the words evoke which thrill, inspire, and uplift my soul in prayer.

November 16

A LULLABY
Sleep, baby, sleep,
The Sun has gone to rest.
Sleep, baby, sleep,
Against thy Mother's breast.
Dream then of love
So tender and so true,
While high above
God watches over you.

Sleep, baby, sleep,
Four angels guard thy bed.
Sleep, baby, sleep,
They bless thy curly head.
And when the sun
Awakes the dreaming earth,
God gives thee fun,
Sunshine and childish mirth.

This is a lullaby I wrote after my second son was born. What mother hasn't said a prayer as she saw her child asleep? So small, so sweet—so vulnerable.

November 17

For the cause that lacks assistance,
For the wrong that needs resistance,
For the future in the distance,
    And the good that I can do.

GEORGE L. BANKS

How difficult it is to support the unpopular cause, to speak out against what one knows in one's heart is wrong. But all reformers great or small suffer the sneers and jeers of disbelievers—until they are proved right.

November 18

Love makes everything lovely; hate concentrates itself on the one thing hated.

GEORGE MACDONALD

November 19

> Why slander we the times?
>   What crimes
> Have days and years, that we
> Thus charge them with iniquity?
>   If we could rightly scan,
> It's not the times are bad, but man.

DR. J. BEAUMONT

"Things ain't what they used to be" is a constant refrain in every age, but it is up to each one of us to ensure that our times are more civilized, more intelligent and more splendid than those in the past.

November 20

The problems which arise in "the daily round, the common task" fall into their proper perspective when we have clearly before us a view of past and present, and, though hazily, a vision of the future.

RONALD CARTLAND

November 21

Break down in us the prison of our false individuality and selfhood,
And unite us with the One who is in us and of whom we are a part.
Teach us to rejoice in our own nobility and to recognize our divinity that, in blindness we may never sin against our true self.
Give us therefore to see death and life as dreams vanishing in the dawn of the soul.

Ancient Wisdom

November 22

Never a tear bedims the eye
That time and patience will not dry:
Never a lip is curved with pain
That can't be kissed into smiles again.

BRETT HART

How important those kisses are! We give kisses today casually without thought, but when they are urgently needed the touch of our lips is the most generous gift we can offer.

November 23

The very names of things beloved are dear,
And sounds will gather beauty from their sense,
As many a face through love's long residence,
Groweth to fair instead of plain and sere.

ROBERT BRIDGES

*When women are in love they become beautiful because love gives them
a radiance which comes from the heart, and also because being in love
they think, feel and see beauty everywhere.*

November 24

*Time is relative. If today one were on a ship which left Southampton a
day ago, that would be yesterday, while New York would be nearly a
week ahead. But if we were high up in the sky, a moon, a star, or
God, Southampton, New York, and this moment would be the
present—today.*

November 25

As unto the bow the cord is,
So unto the man is woman;
Though she bends him, she obeys him,
Though she draws him, yet she follows;
Useless each without the other!

HENRY W. LONGFELLOW

*This is the answer to the battle of the sexes—to the women who seek for
a material equality, to the men who have forgotten how to love with
adoration. Man is useless without woman and woman without man.*

November 26

Once to every man and nation comes the
    moment to decide,
In the strife of Truth with Falsehood,
    for the good or evil side.

J. R. LOWELL

All our studies, our education, our prayers are a preparation for this moment. And how can we fail to make the right choice if God is guiding us?

November 27

For now the unborn God in the human heart
Knows for a moment all sublimities . . . .
Old people at evening sitting in the doorways
See in a broken window of the slum
The Burning Bush reflected, and the crumb
For the starving bird is part of the broken Body
Of Christ who forgives us—He with the bright Hair
—The Sun Whose Body was split on our fields to bring us
harvest.

EDITH SITWELL

November 28

Were we eloquent as angels yet we should please some men, some women, and some children, much more by listening than by talking.

C. C. COLTON

How hard it is to remember we must listen when, as we grow older, we have so much to say! But listeners often help more than those who preach!

November 29

Somebody knows when your heart aches,
And everything seems to go wrong,
Somebody knows when the shadows
Need chasing away with a song;
Somebody knows when you're lonely,
Tired, discouraged, and blue;
Somebody wants you to know Him,
And know that He dearly loves you.

Somebody knows when you're tempted,
And your mind grows dizzy and dim;
Somebody cares when you're weakest,
And farthest away from Him;
Somebody grieves when you've fallen,
You never are lost from His sight;
Somebody waits for your coming,
And He'll drive the gloom from the night.

Somebody loves you when you're weary,
Somebody loves you when you're strong,
Somebody's waiting to help you,
He watches you—one of the throng,
Needing His friendship so holy,
Needing his watchful care so true,
His Name? We call his Name "Jesus"
He loves everyone. He loves you!

November 30

Lord thou knowest how busy I must be today. If I forget thee, do not thou forget me.

Amen.

LORD ASTLEY AT THE BATTLE OF EDGEHILL, 1642

December

December 1

Love all God's creation, the whole world
and every grain of sand. Love every leaf
and every ray of God's light. Love animals
and plants. Love everything. But remember
that you must face the mystery of God in
everything you love.

FEODOR DOSTOEVSKY

*And in ourselves! Even in the worst, most wicked, and the most
bestial, there is still the Spirit of God which is life.*

December 2

When I am dead, my dearest,
 Sing no sad songs for me;
Plant thou no roses at my head,
 Nor shady cypress tree:
Be the green grass above me
 With showers and dewdrops wet;
And if thou wilt, remember,
 And if thou wilt, forget.

CHRISTINA GEORGINA ROSSETTI

*I have always felt that it is un-Christian to mourn too much when
someone dies. We cry for ourselves, not for them, and if we believe in
an afterlife, then they are happy and at peace.*

*Personally, I believe that neither life nor love can die, and although
our bodies wither and decay, the life-force within us goes on.*

*Love is the gift from God, and we move always through eternity
with those we love, in one life after another, perhaps in different
planets, or in different guises.*

What is important, what matters is that there is no death.

180

December 3

He who thinks his place below him
will certainly be below his place.

LORD HALIFAX

December 4

God moves in a mysterious way
    His wonders to perform:
He plants His footsteps in the sea,
    And rides upon the storm.

WILLIAM COWPER

When I look back on my long life I am thrilled by the pattern of it. It is like looking at the wrong side of a Persian carpet, and little actions which seemed to be unimportant at the time have become of great importance as the years pass, not only to me, but to many other people.

How stupid I was to worry or even despair because I thought I had done the wrong thing, when all the time God was moving in His mysterious way, to make it right.

Now I have discovered the beauty of His footsteps as He walks beside me.

December 5

O to bring back the great Homeric time,
The simple manners and the deeds sublime;
When the wise Wanderer, often foiled by Fate,
Through the long furrow drave the ploughshare
straight.

MORTIMER COLLINS

This was a letter written to Disraeli. Today there are still "sublime deeds" if we look for them. There are still those who see straight the way of truth and purpose.

December 6

The characteristics of the English people which have gone to build up the country, which you will still find steadily accumulating all down the ages, illuminating our own history and giving a lead to the whole world, are the characteristics of self-reliance, faith in one's destiny, and courage.

RONALD CARTLAND

December 7

Man is his own star, and the soul that can
Render an honest and a perfect man
Commands all light, all influence, all fate;
Nothing to him falls early or too late.
Our acts our angels are, for good or ill,
Our fatal shadows that walk by us still.

JOHN FLETCHER

We are not only responsible for our actions, we pay for them. Nothing is for free, and once we understand that, we accept it as being just.

December 8

> Here's a sigh to those who love me,
>   And a smile to those who hate;
> And whatever sky's above me,
>   Here's a heart for every fate.
>
> LORD BYRON

This philosophy will make us happy. We cannot expect everyone to like us, but it is not worth worrying about it—just smile!

December 9

> For the human heart is the mirror
>   Of the things that are near and far;
> Like the wave that reflects in its bosom
>   The flower and the distant star.
>
> ALICE CAREY

What do we mirror in our hearts? Wisdom or trivialities, mysteries or frivolities? What we must try to discover is what we give Love.

December 10

When we really fall in love and give our heart to the person we love, we want to believe it is unspoilt, undamaged by what has happened before we met.

This is why we must never accept false love, or the second-rate, but wait for a true and real love to find us.

As history has shown, we may have to wait a long time, but love comes eventually, and when it does all Heaven is ours.

December 11

Life lives for ever; Death of her knows naught,
Our souls through radiant mystery are led.
Clothed in fresh raiment as the old is shed.

LAURENCE BINYON

Here again is a reference to rebirth, a universal belief in the East, and for us an inspirational hope that next time we will do better.

December 12

O Please help me, Dear Lord, to find and win the right *Marriage Partner!* I am so lonely . . . and there is so much love locked away in my heart! Let me find another to whom I may give this sweet love forever and ever!

Each evening at sunset, I long to be in the arms of one who loves me . . . the two of us so Happy in our little home! This is my *fondest dream!*

Amen

December 13

Queen of the World, O Mother Mary!
Potent Virgin, full of Grace!
Shed thy light across the darkness
That enshrouds the human race.
Banish strife and greed and hatred;
Heal the poisoned minds of men;
Vanquish pride and bring God's children
To their Father's Fold again.

Amen

Here is a prayer from Ireland and we should all pray that the strife in that lovely country should cease.

December 14

What is the worth of anything
But for the happiness 'twill bring?

RICHARD OWEN CAMBRIDGE

I have seen a diamond necklace hardly raise a smile of gratitude, and a blind man's face become ecstatic when a child put a flower into his hand.

December 15

Through God, who gave that word of might
    Which swelled creation's lay;
"Let there be light, and there was light."
    What chased the clouds away?
'Twas Love whose finger traced aloud
A bow of promise on the cloud.

MARY BAKER EDDY

The signs of God are always those of light—the Star of Bethlehem, the Burning Bush, the rainbow. However difficult the way, however hard the cross we have to bear, I believe there is always a rainbow.

December 16

Land of Heart's Desire,
Where beauty has no ebb, decay, no flood,
But joy is wisdom, Time an endless song.

WILLIAM BUTLER YEATS

We all dream of a fairyland and imagine we find it! And because dreams do come true we get what we desire.

Not perhaps exactly as we imagined it would be, but we become wise enough to be grateful for what we have and realize how lucky we are to have so much already.

That is where the Land of Heart's Desire actually lies—within our souls.

December 17

God always gives us strength to bear our troubles day by day; but He never calculated on our piling the troubles past, and those to come, on top of those of today.

ELBERT HUBBARD

December 18

Every time a child says: "I don't believe in fairies," there is a little fairy somewhere that falls down dead!

JAMES BARRIE

I sometimes ask myself how often I have killed a fairy in someone's mind by indifference, cynicism and, perhaps worst of all, lack of sympathy, I pray that it will not happen today.

December 19

Far, far below, the moon-blanched olive-trees shone like a silver mist, and the sea glimmered beyond the rock-slopes and the grey precipices and the long, winding path. There was the valley, and the rolled-down stones, which were scattered like the stars in the sky.

Once it was a place of order, where everything was appropriately placed because it was unthinkable that there should be disorder in the presence of Apollo, and so it was again. At night it acquired shape and form and substance. Once again there were the shining palaces of the god on the edge of the cliffs.

The Splendour of Greece

December 20

You can't do without God. He is the only person you can love forever.

FEODOR DOSTOEVSKY

And God will love us for all eternity.

187

December 21

> Life is mostly froth and bubble,
>   Two things stand like stone,
> Kindness in another's trouble
>   Courage in your own.
>
> ADAM LINDSAY GORDON

This is a prayer I have said for many years. It never ceases to inspire me.

December 22

> The moth's kiss, first!
> Kiss me as if you made believe
> You were not sure, this eve,
> How my face, your flower, and pursed
> Its petals up . . . .
> The bee's kiss, now!
> Kiss me as if you entered gay
> My heart at some noonday.
>
> ROBERT BROWNING

A kiss is something so intimate, so personal between two people that I hate to think today how much we debase and spoil such moments of beauty.

The kisses given by sweaty footballers when they kick a goal, the kisses we see given promiscuously on television cheapen what is a treasure to be kept in our hearts.

The kiss of love is both human and divine.

December 23

Seek refuge in inner calm, free your thoughts from the external world and you will feel the rays of God's goodness and love pouring over you and the universe.

IRANSCHAHR

December 24

Even if you cover truth with gold it will gleam in the daylight.
An Old Russian Saying

December 25

Perhaps there is no day in the year when we feel so urgently that we must thank God than Christmas. Deep in our hearts from when we are a child it is a day of praise and gratitude.

The Christmas Story with the shepherds, the angels, the manger, and the Star of Bethlehem overhead is pure magic, and we never grow too old to listen and feel it is a part of our lives that we can never lose.

At Christmas we are all children again with God protecting and guarding us, while every woman feels the maternal love swelling in her heart that Mary had for the Baby Jesus.

All through the year, the love born at Christmas will be with us as surely as there are still stars in the sky to guide us, as one guided the Wise Men.

December 26

Train up a child the way he should go: and when he is old he will not depart from it.

Proverbs

I think this is true, and that is why, whether we have children or not, we must always remember that our example, our actions, our words, and even our thoughts influence the young and affect their lives.

I hear people say: "Oh, I don't matter, I am of no importance." How wrong they are. We all influence those around us, consciously or unconsciously.

O Lord, help me today to say the right thing, that I may help and inspire those with whom I come in contact.

December 27

I awaked in an ancient garden girt fast with four walls of peace. Not a bird-note, not a sound disturbed the profound silence. I lay on the grass dreaming myself back into childhood, the hunter of butterflies, the companion of water rats, rabbits, and all the secret shy creatures haunting the deep green silence of English woods and waters.

I knew where the yellow water lilies raised golden heads above the ripple and the white water lily floated, an embodied prayer with pure chalice and golden heart. I knew where crowding cowslips charmed the meadow grass with their breath of cottage fairies, and where primroses, long-stemmed and with thick leaves larger than rabbit's ears, starred the moss with pale beauty. Of all those things I was dreaming in bliss indescribable, for the child's heart is one with nature.

December 28

In this uncertain, dangerous, difficult world I am certain of only two things; my faith in God and my faith in the English people. There is an instinct in us—our greatest heritage—for what is right and for what is noble. In times of trouble, and in times of happiness, it has never failed us. We have so much to be thankful for, so much to do. God grant that you and I—and England—will never fail.

RONALD CARTLAND

December 29

Never are we so poor as men want to make us. Always we have the wealth which we are, the beauty which we have.

ERNST TOLLER

December 30

Most Holy Mary, my Lady, to thy faithful care and special keeping and to the bosom of thy mercy, today and every day, and particularly at the hour of my death, I commend my soul and my body. All my hope and consolation, all my trials and miseries, my life, and the end of my life I commit to thee, that through thy most holy intercession and by thy merits all my actions may be directed according to thy will and that of thy divine Son.

Amen

This is a prayer to the Mother of God and I feel it is one which will help and comfort all women, especially those who are growing older—as I am.

December 31

Now the New Year reviving old desires
The thoughtful Soul to Solitude retires.

EDWARD FITZGERALD

This is the night we all pray that next year will be a happy one; that we will do better in thought, word, and deed, and that we may find love.

That is what we all need in the year to come—love. We will receive love and we will give it, for without it there is no real happiness.